THE THIRD WAY

by
MARY ANN CLARK

ISBN: 9781791761622

ACKNOWLEDGMENTS

Marne and the people of the Babapupa Reserve have been roaming around my subconscious for a long time. I am happy to finally release the first of what I hope to be several of their stories in my Force of Destiny series.

I owe a special thanks to the members of my critique groups, Richard Boich, Judith March Davis (*Pagoda Dreamer* and *It Seemed to Matter*), Edward Gates (*Ranger's Quest: The Beginning* and *A Ranger's Time*), William Johnstone (*The Seventh Message*), Marian Powell, Dougal Reeves, and Jeff Zucker. Along the way other friends have also read and commented on portions of this story. I especially appreciate my sister Peggy Pavlik's insightful comments.

I owe special thanks to my spouse, Art Gorski who has supported me through all the twists and turns our lives of taken. I couldn't have done any of this without you, babe.

And, of course, this work would never have been finished and published without the invaluable work of my editor, Sandy Vernon, and the cover art of Mariah Sinclair.

CONTENTS

CHAPTER 1

September 2198, Verdant Valley, Babapupa Reserve

Marne fingered the handful of cowries in her pocket. The shells were part of her earnings as Lola's apprentice during the past summer season. At age sixteen, the pleasure of having her own money spread through her, causing the silly grin she had been wearing the entire day.

She waited with her grandmother as her boss, Titilola, activated the bot that would protect the store while they were gone. Lola's scowl and the way she slammed the shop door told Marne the older woman was not as pleased.

"What's the matter?" Marne's granny asked, linking her arm with Lola's. The two women had been friends for a long time.

"Everyone's profits are down again this year," Lola grumbled as the three of them walked away. "Some people think I should have done more." She shook her head, tiny wrinkles furrowing the smooth tan of her forehead.

Lola was the head of the Verdant Valley Market Board and the owner of a popular tourist shop on the town square. She stood a head shorter than most people, but Marne knew no one should underestimate the force of her personality. Marne had observed her throughout the summer. She thought of all the times she had managed the shop alone so Lola could deal with some emergency among the market members. What more could she have done?

"Those people are wrong," Marne's granny said. "It's not your fault the rains didn't come or that we didn't have as many visitors. Besides," she patted Lola's arm, "no one else wants your job. They just want to complain."

As they walked in silence, Marne thought about her first summer as a "little bird." She was at the time in a girl's life when she'd finished her schooling and was moving toward her future as a wife and mother. Although Lola kept Marne busy, she'd found time to flirt and play at being an adult with the boys and unmarried men who hung around the Market. Marne knew most of the young men in her small farming community. The boys her age had been immature and clumsy with her. But the older boys were much more sophisticated as they introduced her to the games men and women played together. Many of those young men had finished their own apprenticeships and would soon be able to offer someone her bride price. Maybe one of them would come for her.

She smiled as she thought of Dele, the son of a prosperous compound. He was one of those older men. They became special friends over the last couple weeks of the summer season. A shiver ran through her when she remembered the things he taught her as they lay together in his hideaway on the edge of the forest. She knew many of the other girls envied his interest in her. She wondered why, when he could afford any girl's price, he still wasn't married. Perhaps she would be the lucky one he chose.

Almost skipping along behind the two older women, Marne realized that she was becoming an adult in other ways as well. As Lola's assistant she was also a member of the Market Board. The society included the local market women and shop owners as well as the farmers and ranchers that made Verdant Valley the breadbasket of the Babapupa Reserve. Today, most people would pay their obligations for the year and pick their officers for the coming year. Lola had led the Board for as long as Marne could remember. She also represented the Board on the village council where the heads of all the groups and circles worked with the *obanla*, their ruler, to manage town affairs.

"You're right, of course, Gladys," Lola said to Marne's granny as they approached the Market Hall. It was a nondescript building except for a vibrant painting on the front wall of Oya, the patron goddess of the Board. The painting depicted Oya as a beautiful dark-skinned woman in a traditional Africa-style wrapper and head tie, presiding over a booth in the market. "No one wants this responsibility," Lola continued. "Sometimes I wonder why I want it myself, but here we are."

As they entered the Hall, Marne bent to drop her offering of cowrie shells into the basket on the Eleggua shrine by the door. Again, pleasure tingled through her. For the first time in her life, she could contribute from her own earnings.

Chairs arranged in semi-circles around a central open area filled the large meeting room. In the opening between the points of the crescents were ornate chairs for the board officers.

Once inside the hall the three women parted. Marne's granny moved to a chair in the innermost circle with the older women and men who were the prominent members of the group. Marne found a seat along the back wall with the other young apprentices. She smiled at several of her friends who also had that glow of the completion of a successful season. Lola took the long way around the hall, weaving in and out among the chairs. Always the politician, Lola hugged and patted many of the people gathered in the hall. Finally, she and the other officers made their way to the ornate chairs in the front of the room.

Looking around as though taking roll, Lola said, "I think we're all here. Close the doors." Then she turned toward the altar behind her chair. Splashing water from a bowl on the floor onto the large porcelain jar in front of her, Lola chanted: "*Omi Tutu, Ani Tutu, Ile Tutu, Egun Tutu, Laroye Tutu, Aiku Baba Wa.*" Marne translated in her head. May cool water bless us. May a cool road lead us. May cool relatives surround us. May a cool house envelop us. May cool Ancestors watch over us. May the owner of gossip never lead us astray. May the ancestors bring their blessings to us.

Lola picked up a bell and rang it as she continued to pray. Then she called, "*Ashé.*" The people in the room echoed, "*Ashé.*" So be it.

Turning back toward the group, Lola sat and activated a screen so everyone could see it. It was a short but serious agenda. "Our first order of business is collecting the obligations." She pulled a large bag from under her chair. "For myself, the shop, my artisans, and my apprentice." She deposited the token bag of cowries in the center of the circle. "Forty thousand, five hundred and sixty-five."

A woman sitting on Lola's right activated her own screen. She verified the amount had been moved from Lola's bank account to the Board's. Lola's *baala*, her second-in-command, pulled out a bag of cowries from under her chair and deposited it in the center of the circle. "For myself, the shop, my artisans, and my two apprentices. Twenty-five thousand, eight hundred and twenty-eight."

The treasurer nodded.

The next highest ranked woman stood up and deposited a bag in the center of the circle. "For myself, the shop, and my artisans. Twenty thousand, three hundred and forty."

As the women continued to step forward to pay their obligations, Marne thought about the history of her home. The Babapupa Reserve was founded when the old United States of America had disintegrated into many small nations. The Reserve was one of the many semi-autonomous reservations sprinkled throughout the Republic of the Great American Southwest. Almost two centuries ago, their African American ancestors colonized a portion of the central Arizona highlands. They wanted to follow their traditions and live according to the old ways. Life in the old desert states of Arizona, Utah, Nevada, New Mexico and northern Mexico was hard for everyone. But the Reserve flourished, buoyed by the influx of Republic dollars brought by the visitors from oppressive desert areas to the south.

Marne and her family lived in an outlying village of Babapupa. At a lower altitude than the capital city of Scarlet Dawn, the area around Verdant Valley was home to the best farm and ranch land in Babapupa. In a normal year, they not only provided food for the Reserve but were able to sell their excess to the rich elites of Phoenix City, the Republic capital. But they had not had a normal season for several years. Lower harvests meant less surplus to sell to outsiders. As the principal shopper for her own household, Marne knew that if this year's harvest was down, everyone would do some belt-tightening.

"Thank you, everyone, for your hard work and generosity." Lola finished up the first agenda item. Marne looked at the piles of bags and baskets representing everyone's contributions. Some of what was collected would be transferred from the Board's account to the village council's. The rest would be used to maintain this hall and continue the work of the Board. The mound looked enormous to Marne, but she had not been listening as the board members declared their contributions. Besides, this was her first year as an apprentice member. Perhaps the total wasn't so very much.

Lola cleared her throat. The agenda shimmered as the first item was checked off. Now would come the more difficult part of the meeting, the election of officers. Some disgruntled members wanted to discharge Lola and her officers and vote in a new set of leaders. Lola listened to the concerns of those who opposed her. There were two main groups with two different set of worries. One group thought she had been in power too long. They said someone newer and younger would be able to reenergize the Board and turn around the losses suffered over the past several years. Marne wondered who they imagined could make the rains come and the visitors return. A second group said Lola took too many chances.

Supporting Lola's efforts on their behalf, Talé, the manager of the largest and most prosperous agricultural complex in the valley, stood up. She made a short presentation of their plan to add goats and sheep to their cattle herds. The idea was to use both the meat and other products from animals that needed fewer resources than cattle. If the herd prospered, it would bring new money to the valley. This was a multi-year plan that had not yet proven itself. Some people opposed the funds designated for such efforts.

As the market members and artisans presented their grievances and opinions, Marne realized her granny had been right. Most of the members seemed to approve of Lola's middle path between stability and change.

They supported the way Lola encouraged innovation without putting too much of their economy at risk. When all the votes had been tallied and verified by the *baala*, Lola's team were re-elected by a comfortable margin.

Lola often talked to Marne about her ability to influence the Board, bringing them along to follow her lead. Now Marne had watched that ability in action. She was amazed. Based on the uneasy conversations she overheard between Lola and her granny and the talk among the other women, Marne would have predicted that the Board would begin the new year with a different leadership group. But she would have been wrong. Once again Lola would be their leader.

Later Marne would look back on this meeting and wonder whether perhaps Lola might have preferred to have lost this fight and let someone else face the menace waiting for them.

After yesterday's Market Board meeting and the end of the summer season, Marne was helping Lola shut down the shop for the winter. There would be few visitors until next spring. Many market women sold their merchandise from booths on the central square; however, Lola rented a permanent location along the main street. The principal industry of Verdant Valley was agriculture, but *oyinbo* from the south visited the town as well. One draw for those visitors were the handmade items produced and sold by the people of the Reserve. Lola sold the cloth Marne's granny dyed out at her workshop, clothing for women and children, and other soft goods. She also had one-of-a-kind jewelry and trinkets.

Today she and Marne were sorting through the inventory. Together they decided what needed to be returned to the artisans and what should be moved to Lola's storage facility for the winter. Unsalable items they would put on a table outside for the people known as the condors, the poorest of the poor. Marne projected the holographic inventory into the air between them so either one could update the records.

Once they moved the inventory out and cleaned up the shop, Lola would decide if it needed any changes or repairs. Based on Marne's understanding of the low profits for the season, she doubted that much repair work would be done this year. That meant she would fulfill her obligation as Lola's apprentice in the next couple of days and be ready to begin her winter work.

Marne's grandmother was a dyer of extraordinary indigo cloth. Winter was when Granny and her apprentices worked the dye pots making new cloth for next summer's season. It was hot, difficult work, made easier by the cooler temperatures. When Marne was younger, her granny let her hang around the workshop when she wasn't in school, running errands and the like. Last winter as she was finishing up her classes, she was allowed to work part-time as an apprentice. Now she looked forward to returning full-time. She thought about how hard the work had been. She returned home every afternoon dirty and exhausted. But she so loved the cloth, and she was eager to learn more about turning plain cloth into the intricate indigo patterns that were her granny's specialty. She hoped to work a couple more years before she got married and moved away from Verdant Valley and her family.

"The Council meets in eight days," Lola said as they worked. "Since I was re-elected yesterday, I'll be representing the Board again. I want you to come with me." Lola turned to look at Marne. "I want to train you to become my assistant. Josephine, my current assistant, is getting married in the spring and will be moving to Scarlet Dawn."

Marne knew the Verdant Valley Council was made up of representatives of the most important groups in the village. It was led by the *obanla,* whom outsiders often mistakenly called their king. He wasn't really a king, but the most senior man in the village. He was appointed by the powerful Council of Elders to be their leader. As the head of the Market Board, Lola was also the Board's representative.

"You have done a good job this summer, and I'd like you to continue working with me." Lola gave Marne the same warm smile she used to convince the market members to elect her to another term as their head. Marne felt the same tenderness those women must have felt.

"But, but …" Marne sputtered despite her feelings for her mentor. Lola knew now she had graduated she wanted to work with her granny. They had talked about Marne's plans and prospects. If she wanted to have her own workshop someday, she needed to learn as much as she could before marriage took her away.

Lola held up her hand as if deflecting Marne's objections. "I know. I know. You are planning on working with Gladys over the winter."

Marne nodded. She was looking forward to a winter working out at her granny's workshop.

"Gladys and I have talked about it," Lola continued. "The council isn't very busy this time of year and we think we can share you. You can be my assistant-in-training over the winter and her apprentice."

Marne continued to stare at Lola amazed. Dyeing cloth was hard work. Many of the girls that started as her granny's apprentices didn't last the whole season. They gave up and lost the promised bolt of material that was their season's end bonus. Even if she was no longer in school, how could Lola and her granny expect her to work for both of them? She shook her head. She and her sister were still responsible for her family's apartment, since their father's new wife refused to do any cooking or cleaning. Marne did not think she could work the dye pots, help keep her father's apartment, and continue working for Lola. It was just too much.

"Being my assistant won't be a great deal of work. You'll share the job with Josephine. By the time she gets married next spring, you'll be almost finished at Gladys's workshop. If you can't be my assistant and work the shop next summer, I'll find someone else for the shop." Lola stepped forward. "I like the work you've done for me, and Gladys and I both think this is a great opportunity for you."

Marne's opposition melted in the glow of Lola's praise and before she could protest further Lola released her. "Let's finish up here, then go over to the *obanla's* compound where my offices are. You know Josephine. She can show you around, introduce you to the other assistants, and get you set up. Then you can take tomorrow off and start with Josephine the following day."

Without waiting for Marne's reply, Lola turned back to the clothing she had been sorting. She held up a popular baby outfit. "I think we can keep this for next summer, don't you?"

Marne nodded, agreeing both to Lola's question and her demand that Marne become her assistant.

As soon as Marne walked through the gates of her family compound, her friend Anana waved to her from across the courtyard.

"Hey, girl. Over here!" Anana was a heavy-set young woman who emanated love for herself, her family, and her friends. She sat with her eighteen-month-old son, Karamat, taking in the final bit of sunlight as night approached. Marne fell into the chair beside them.

"Marne, Marne!" Little Kara, as everyone called the child, reached out toward her. She took him from his mother. He was as roly-poly as his mother and just as lovable. Marne kissed and tickled him until he was giggling uncontrollably, then settled him on her lap, where he played with the tips of her braids.

Anana gestured toward the beer on the table between them. "We should celebrate your first day on the job."

The two women picked up the beer mugs and clinked them together. Marne's granny said she was too young to be drinking beer, but Marne had been sharing this time with Anana throughout the summer. Besides, she was feeling quite grown up after her first day as Lola's assistant. Marne always enjoyed the way the golden liquid slid down her throat and infused her with warmth. Today she was also grateful for this small respite before taking on her domestic responsibilities. She and Perla, her sister, shared the running of her father's household, including the shopping and cooking for themselves, their father, and his new wife. This morning they had agreed that Perla would manage today's housework, so Marne could take a few minutes with Anana before going home.

7

"So, how do you feel, being the assistant to the most difficult woman on the council?" Anana teased.

"Assistant-in-training," Marne responded. "And she's not that difficult. Remember, I've been working for her all summer." Lola had been hard on Marne at the beginning of the season until Marne showed her she was a fast learner. She thought they worked well together. Lola must agree. Otherwise, why would she ask Marne to be her assistant?

"Wait and see," Anana winked. "Wait until she gets into it with her husband or another council member. Then you'll see."

"Josephine said she liked her and I've never had any problems." Marne was surprised that she felt she needed to defend her boss. "And everyone seemed cordial today." It hadn't been a difficult day for Marne even though everything in the back rooms of the council chambers in the *obanla's* compound was new and strange. The council meeting she sat through had gone smoothly. Everyone acted just as she expected them to act.

Anana laughed. "Today all they wanted to do was tie up the loose ends from the summer season and get ready for their fall recess." She lifted her mug and took a drink. "Just you wait. It won't be long before you see the Bobcat in action."

"The Bobcat?" Marne shifted little Kara into a more comfortable position.

"That's what Malik calls her—behind her back, of course."

Malik was the *obanla*, the head of the village council and the most powerful man in Verdant Valley. He was also Anana's boss. She became one of his many assistants over four years ago when she'd moved to Verdant Valley to marry one of Marne's cousins.

"Because …?" Marne acted like she didn't understand.

"She's small but tough. Not afraid to take on anyone, even the *obanla* himself." Anana rolled her eyes, then smiled. "I've seen him back down in the face of her attack—more than once."

Marne knew Lola had no problems standing up for herself, but to the *obanla*? She must be ferocious. This job might be more fun than she thought. She took another sip of beer, then looked at Anana. "That won't cause problems between us, will it?" Anana was her best friend, the older sister she didn't have.

"Oh, no. I admire her and … she's usually right." She winked again. "I wouldn't tell Malik that, of course. And if you say anything …" She let the mock threat hang between them.

"Of course." Marne held out her hand, and they hooked pinkies like two little girls taking a vow.

"What about her husband, Akande? Doesn't he support her?"

Anana looked like her beer had gone bad. "No. He, he…" she stuttered, obviously looking for the right words. She started again. "If you only saw the two of them at the office, you'd never know they were married. You would think the Traders Board representative would be a natural ally of the Market Board's rep, even if they weren't married. But…" again she paused. "But, he's not." She grew silent for a moment, then continued. "Be careful around him." Anana became serious, as if she was afraid of what she was saying. "He's not what he appears to be, and he is no champion of Lola's. Stay away from him and try to stay away from his people."

Little Kara jumped off Marne's lap and scampered across the plaza toward Anana's apartment.

"That's my cue," Anana said. "Remember, you're one of the Bobcat's kits. She'll protect you."

Marne watched her friend disappear into her apartment. Everything seemed so amicable in the *obanla's* compound today, but now she was beginning to see there was more going on under the surface. However, being Lola's assistant, one of her "kits" as Anana said, offered her some protection. At least she hoped so.

CHAPTER 2

Marne waited in the sitting room of her father's apartment. She had bathed and dressed in her finest white wrapper and head tie. Now she waited for Jumoke, her godmother, to accompany her to the forest home to the principal Orisha shrines. In the years since Jumoke had initiated Marne into the worship of Yemaya, the Great Mother Goddess, she had gone to the shrine many times both alone and accompanied by others. It had not been long before Marne discovered she could be one of Yemaya's speakers, the mediums through which the goddess communicated to her devotees. In the years since the Orisha first spoke through her, she had often given up herself so Yemaya could speak through her.

But today she was not just attending a ritual where she might be one of many through whom the goddess spoke. Today, she was the designated medium, the priest chosen to be the principal dancer and the principal voice of the Orisha. Today's ritual was a test, an audition. The senior priests would see whether she could allow Yemaya to slip into herself on demand. Then they would ask Yemaya to confirm Marne as one of Her chosen ones, as one of Her designated speakers. If Yemaya validated her, then she would dance and speak at the public rituals on the village square and in the formal ceremonial hall. She would become one of the public faces of the goddess.

Marne heard Jumoke knock on the front door of the apartment, but before she could respond, her godmother let herself in.

"Are you ready?" Jumoke asked as she reached the doorway where Marne stood in the middle of the room. Jumoke was a spry older woman with skin the color of wet desert sand and close-cropped hair that looked like a silvery cloud around her head. She had been the first priest Marne met when she went to the Yemaya shrine not long after her mother's death. As her godmother, Jumoke had been Marne's guide to becoming a priest herself.

"Good, good." Jumoke circled her, patting this and that loose edge. "Are you nervous?"

"N-no," Marne lied, trying to act brave.

"Well, I am," her godmother admitted. "This is a big step for you." Then she stepped in front of the girl and hugged her. "You'll do fine. Yemaya loves you and said She wanted this from you years ago."

With that assurance, Jumoke put her arm around Marne's waist and led her out of the apartment, through the compound courtyard, and down the street toward the local market. After they bought the required offerings, she led Marne away from the village center and into the sacred forest with its Orisha shrines.

Even before Jumoke knocked on her father's door, Marne had begun to feel that mental fog she knew was often the lightest touch of the Orisha. She was glad that Jumoke had insisted they go to today's ritual together. Even though she had made this trip many times, Marne was not sure she would have been able to buy the offering or even find her way through the forest to Yemaya's shrine alone today. It was reassuring that the Orisha was already touching her. That would make it easier for Marne to let go during the ritual.

The Orisha had possessed Marne many times. However, the senior priests never asked Yemaya to name Marne as an official speaker. She was too young, they said, too inexperienced. Marne accepted their judgment but Jumoke did not. Her godmother had insisted on this test of her abilities.

"Yemaya asked for this one to be a speaker the first time she danced for the goddess," Jumoke said when the two of them had stood before the shrine's governing council. "How long are you going to deny Yemaya's will?"

So now the day had come to prove herself, to them, and to the Great Mother.

When they got to the shrine, Jumoke led Marne through the courtyard filled with the odors of the meal that would be served after the ritual, then through the gathering room where the drummers were warming up. She opened the door to the small space that served as the speaker's dressing room.

"Wait here," Jumoke said. "I will come for you when we're ready."

As she sat and waited, Marne listened to the other priests and worshippers gathering. She sang along with the opening refrain to Eleggua, the trickster Orisha, who was always the first to be invoked. She listened for the beginning of the Yemaya chant that would be her cue to join the other worshippers. As she became light-headed, she leaned over, putting her head between her knees. It would not do for her to appear wobbly or unsure when the time came.

Marne felt the fog that had enveloped her all morning lift. Thank the Goddess, she could do this without embarrassing herself or her godmother. She lifted her head and opened her eyes and saw the most senior priests surrounding. Where was she? She was not in the speaker dressing room anymore and she was no longer wearing Yemaya's costume.

"Here, take a drink, dear." Jumoke wrapped Marne's hand around a glass and guided it to her lips. She smelled the herbal beverage before tasting it. It was the same drink they gave her after every time she spoke for Yemaya.

As her head cleared, Marne realized the Orisha must have taken her in the dressing room and that she had danced already. Had Yemaya accepted, then? She looked her question into Jumoke's eyes.

"Yes, yes," her godmother said, guiding the glass back toward Marne's mouth. "Yemaya spoke through you and accepted you as her speaker. But she said much more. When you have recovered, we'll talk about it."

The others stepped away. They must have realized that she had come back from her possession.

"Come to the small shrine room, when you are ready," the high priestess's voice said somewhere behind her. "We need to discuss this in the presence of Yemaya."

The others murmured their agreement. The door opened, and then closed, leaving Marne and Jumoke alone.

"Did I dance?" Marne asked, although from the light coating of sweat and the ache in her muscles she knew the answer.

Jumoke nodded. "You danced more beautifully than I have ever see anyone dance for Yemaya."

"And she accepted me?"

Jumoke nodded again. "As we knew she would." She smiled. "Yemaya said she loves you very much. She has been waiting for you to ask her permission to be her speaker for a long time."

Marne grinned, then sobered. "But something else happened, didn't it?"

"Yes, Yemaya said many things through you, many dark and ominous things." This time Jumoke frowned. "As the speaker, you are entitled to know what she said. When you're ready, we will meet with the others to try to understand what Yemaya is asking of us."

The Orisha often spoke in proverbs from the divination texts as Yemaya had done today. The priests explained Yemaya's statement to the assembled congregation. It could be summed up in the warning found in number 12-3 of the *Diloggun*, the divination text: "Enemies, war, and afterwards well-being." Without context such a warning was meaningless. All the assembled priests were experienced diviners and interpreters of the utterances of the Orisha. Yet none could decipher the statement Marne-as-Yemaya said over and over again, screaming, whispering, weeping, laughing. No wonder Marne's throat and palms ached. She had spent hours yelling at the gathered group and pounding on the walls. No one had been able to either calm her or convince her to explain what Yemaya was telling them.

Sitting with the leaders of the shrine, Marne saw she was the youngest person there, both in actual age — she was barely sixteen, still wearing the waist beads of an unmarried woman — and in terms of her priesthood. They had celebrated her third religious birthday a mere month ago. She was only allowed to join this group because she had been Yemaya's mouthpiece. Her godmother had brought her out of her trance, but she still felt the tingle of Yemaya's presence. It was the tingle she sometimes felt when she was doing divination for a client, the tingle that reminded her the Orisha was always a part of her.

"If someone came to me for divination and 12-3 fell," Marne croaked out when there was a pause in the discussion. Her throat still hurt. "I'd have to assume something is going on my client either hadn't told me or didn't know about."

They all stared at her as if she was a child interrupting an adult conversation. She had no idea where she was going but she pushed forward. "I'm thinking we're all the client. We came here with one question but we've received an unexpected answer that doesn't seem to have any relevance to our original question."

They were listening to Marne now and nodding. Every diviner had seen such a thing.

"I'm not an experienced diviner," she said, "so in a case like this I might come to one or another of you for advice." More nodding. "What would you tell me?"

Marne looked around, focusing first on her granny, the one who first brought her to this shrine. Then, nodding to her godmother who initiated her not that long ago, she stepped into the silence enveloping the room. "You have taught me everything I know about listening to the Orisha and understanding what they have to say to us." Her voice quivered at her daring. The others looked at her but the power of Yemaya still flowed through her. "I think you would tell me to ask if there was a war brewing within the client, their family, or their compound. Is there a war brewing in the shrine?"

As she looked from one to another she saw them considering her question. There were always squabbles among the priests, the squabbles typical of any group trying to work together. Were any of these disagreements rising to the level of war? Was there something under the surface here that the Great Mother had to issue such a dire warning? The priests looked at one another.

Finally, Olamide, the high priestess, spoke up. "As you well know, there are always petty rivalries among us, but I know of nothing that could be called a war." She watched the others nod, agreeing with her assessment.

"Then," Marne continued, her voice stronger, "we must look beyond this shrine. Do any of you know of a war brewing elsewhere in Verdant Valley?"

Again the priests considered her question, shaking their heads as they pondered what they knew from their various lives. Arguments between compounds and among the different groups and factions within the village were common. Were any of these clashes likely to lead to war?

It was Olamide who answered her. "The village, too, is home to quarrels and disagreements, but I don't know of any war brewing." She looked around.

"Nor I," said one.

"Nothing," said another.

The whisper of their objections flowed through the group.

"You need to talk to the other shrines, the other groups, perhaps even the village council itself." She swallowed, still surprised at her own daring. "Yemaya is telling us war is coming. We must be prepared."

The room was silent, then exploded in a cacophony of voices. Marne sat back, exhausted by the events of the afternoon. She no longer tingled with the energy of the Orisha. She had said all that Yemaya required of her.

Olamide clapped her hands, regaining control of her priests. "*Modupue*, Yarawode." She thanked Marne, using her ritual name. "I believe you continued to speak with the voice of Yemaya and have given us wise counsel." She turned to Marne's godmother. "Get her something to eat, while we consider what should be done."

Helping Marne to her feet, Jumoke led her from the room. Pressing some cowries into her hand, Jumoke led her toward the large Yemaya shrine room. "One last thing before you can get your just reward of some food," she said. "You must thank Yemaya for her blessings this day."

Marne's elation at being accepted as Yemaya's speaker was tempered by the message she had given and the uncertainty surrounding it. Then she remembered the speaker was not responsible for the words of the Orisha. Olamide and the others would discuss this with the *obanla* and his council. They would know what to do. She was relieved that she would not be involved in whatever was coming for them.

"Thank you, Yemaya," she prayed as she made her offering. "Thank you for accepting me as your speaker and for letting me continue to work with both Lola and Granny. You have given me many blessings and I am grateful. *Modupue*. Thank you."

CHAPTER 3

Two days after her visit to the shrine and her acceptance as Yemaya's speaker, Marne was back to work as Lola's assistant.

"Don't work too late tonight," Lola told Marne as she prepared to leave the *obanla's* compound for the day. The day's council session had run much over its assigned time and Marne felt the pressure to complete her work before going home.

"I won't," Marne said. "I have a couple things I want to finish. Then I'll be leaving, too."

Tapping the top of her desk, Marne projected the next page of her report in the air in front of her. One thing she had learned while working in Lola's shop was how much work she got done when fewer people were around. Josephine assured her that working late in the council's wing of the compound was not a problem. The Hunters Guild patrolled the hallways until the council members and their staff vacated the space and they could lock the outside door.

Marne remained dimly aware of doors closing as the others left. Soon all she could hear was the distant hum of the rest of the *obanla's* compound. Just as she was doing the final readthrough of the report that Lola wanted to have first thing in the morning, Marne heard steps outside her office. She turned to greet the guild member she thought was checking to be sure she had not gone off and left on her light.

"I'm just about to go," she said, glancing toward the doorway.

To her surprise, it wasn't a hunter but Akande, Lola's husband, and the representative of the Traders Board. He was a tall, slender man who wore the white dress shirt and slacks of the *oyinbo*, the strangers who lived down in the City. He had risen to the leadership of the Board on his reputation as the best negotiator when dealing with their *oyinbo* partners. Where many people found Malik, the *obanla*, difficult to work with, Akande was friendly and outgoing, just the person to oil the wheels of commerce with the outside world.

"Working late, Little Bird?" He pulled the door closed behind him.

"Just finished." She closed her display and signed off the council's private network.

"Excellent." He smiled at her. "I've been watching you. You're a very dedicated worker. Just look, you're the last one to quit."

She nodded, trying to return his smile.

He stared as she stood up and collected her things. Her arms were full of several bags of household items she'd picked up from the market earlier.

"I've been wanting to talk to you," Akande said. "Could you come by my office for a moment?"

Without waiting for her answer, he turned, opened the door again, and walked from her office and down the hall. She closed and locked her door, then followed him. When he pushed his door open, she saw he had not led her to his working office but to his sitting room.

Although smaller than the room where she and Lola met with the *obanla* and members of the Market Board, Akande's had the same large meeting table and several smaller seating groups. He lowered the lights as they walked toward a pair of easy chairs with a small table and a single lamp between them. The dim light illuminated only that area, leaving the remainder of the room in the shadows. Marne jumped when she heard the door close behind her. She was uneasy, but he was a councilman and Lola's husband.

By the time she piled her things next to one chair and sat, he had produced a bottle of wine and two glasses.

"How old are you?" he asked, a hint of a wolfish smile tugging at his lips.

"Sixteen," she stammered. Her granny said she was too young to drink. That hadn't stopped her from sharing glasses of beer with some of the flirty boys in the market and with Anana after work.

"You are just a little bird," Akande said. "I bet your father has marriage prospects lined up outside his door." He poured wine into the glasses and handed her one.

She shook her head, refusing the wine.

"No? Well, he should. Here, take this," he commanded. "It's mild. You'll like it."

He lifted his glass toward her in a salute, waiting for her to do likewise. When she tentatively raised her glass, he nodded. "To your future," he said, taking a deep gulp and emptying the glass.

Marne put the glass to her lips and took a sip.

"No, no," he said. "You don't get the full flavor unless you fill your mouth and hold it."

She took a bigger drink, holding it in her mouth as he instructed.

"Now, swallow," he said, nodding encouragement.

She did as she he said, coughing at the bitterness of the liquid. This tasted nothing like the beer she was used to.

"Good," he laughed. "Now again, this time you won't need to cough."

Taking another drink, she held it. Then she swallowed, clenching her throat tight to keep from coughing again. She stared at him, uncertain of why she was there.

He refilled their glasses, then sat back and watched her take another drink. This time the wine traced a warm path into her stomach and beyond.

"Such a pretty little bird," he murmured more to himself than to her. His voice was a soft caress and her unease receded.

After a moment, Marne felt as though everything was turning fuzzy and Akande was very far away. Clumsily she set the glass back on the table without spilling the remaining wine. This wasn't right.

"I-I need to be going." She made a half-hearted attempt to stand.

"Wait," he said. "We're not done yet."

"No," she said, pushing herself up and almost losing her balance as she leaned over to collect her things.

She felt Akande watching as she wove her way across the room. Before she could figure out how to open the door, she felt his arms around her. A faint musky aroma she hadn't noticed earlier surrounded her.

"Here, let me help you," he whispered, brushing his moist lips against her earlobe.

She shuddered as he reached around her to push the door open, his arm brushing against her breast.

"Another evening, perhaps," he said, releasing her to stumble down the hall. "Good night, my Little Bird."

The next day Marne tried to stay out of Akande's path. She planned to only work late when Lola or Josephine also worked late. If she passed him in the hallway or in one of the council meeting rooms, she stayed as far from him as she could. She soon learned that was not always possible, as several times he moved close enough to brush his fingertips against her as he passed.

The hardest came at midday when Akande had his weekly lunch for the staff. On Market Days, many of the other council members met with their boards and circles. However, Akande held lunch for their assistants and aides in his largest private sitting room. These luncheons were training opportunities for the assistants, a chance to learn more about the history and governance of the Babapupa Reserve and Verdant Valley.

Her first week of work Marne was invited to these gatherings. As the newest of the assistants, Lola said, it would be good for her to attend. While Lola and Josephine met with the Market Board, Marne became part of the group of assistants having lunch with Akande and Louis, his chief of staff.

Like his boss, Louis was a middle-aged man always dressed in the *oyinbo* style. With his starched white shirt, tie, and vest, he looked ready to confer with Akande's trading partners in the far-away Phoenix City. After her encounter in Akande's sitting room, Marne was leery of being in such a small group with him. But she could not think of a reason not to attend his luncheon today. Since she was running late, she was the last to arrive.

"Here, come sit by me." Akande pointed next to him on the sofa, the only open space in the circle of assistants. Marne wanted to keep her distance, but over the course of the luncheon Akande spread himself out until his leg and arm touched hers. As he drew closer, she smelled his musky aroma. It reminded her of those afternoons she had spent with Dele in his secret hideaway at the edge of the forest.

As the meeting progressed, he directed several questions to her, too. When she responded correctly, he grinned as though she was his own special project. Most disconcerting, he went from calling her "Little Bird," a term of endearment many older people used to refer to girls who had put on their waist beads but were not yet married, to calling her "My Little Bird," implying there was a relationship between them.

Much to her relief, she survived the luncheon without incident and, whatever the other assistants thought, no one said anything to her about Akande. However, she noticed Louis leering as she moved through the warren of rooms that formed the *obanla*'s offices. She vowed to avoid both men while continuing her work.

That evening Marne tried to talk to her friend Anana about her discomfort around Akande. She had wanted to avoid another one-on-one meeting with him but he seemed to be everywhere, leering at her.

"You're right to be concerned," Anana said. "Everyone knows he likes the young girls fresh into their womanhood. There are always rumors swirling around him. Some people say he's got an *oyinbo* family down in the City. Or an *alekere* or second wife over in Scarlet Dawn. I don't know if any of those rumors are true, but Akande likes for people to think he is a big man. Lola knows how he is but she doesn't like it. If she thinks you're the one fooling around with him, she'll fire you in an instant. Stay away from him."

Marne nodded. She didn't want to have anything to do with Akande, but she did not know how to avoid him.

I need to quit going to his lunches, she thought. Tomorrow she would ask Josephine about accompanying her and Lola when they met with the market women. She needed to learn that part of her job, after all, and then she could turn down further invitations from Akande.

She nodded to Anana. "You're right," Marne said. "I don't want to jeopardize my relationship with Lola."

CHAPTER 4

"And with that, …" Malik's closing remarks were drowned out by noises out in the courtyard. It sounded to Marne like the loudest motorcycles she had ever heard were idling outside the council's meeting room.

Members of the council gaped at each other as Raymon, the *baala*, jumped up and strode over to the door. As he approached, it slammed open and two *oyinbo*, pale-skinned men from outside the Reserve, stomped in. They wore black leather jackets and trousers and carried dark motorcycle helmets with images of snake-like demons embossed on the side. Bandoliers full of bullets crisscrossed their chests.

"Wh-what…" Malik began but before he could continue the larger of the two very large men pushed him aside.

"Where is the rest of our tribute, Worms?" the man roared, leaning over the council table.

"Y-your tr-tribute is in the u-usual pl-place, Ma-Master D-duke." Marne barely understood Akande's response.

Standing off to the side, Malik pulled himself together, then stood behind Akande so he could face the man Akande called Master Duke. "We were told the trucks were loaded and waiting for you," his voice faltered but he continued. "Is there a problem?"

"You scum are trying to cheat us." Master Duke spat onto the table between Akande's hands. "Where is the rest of our tribute?"

"The rest…" Malik began.

"Listen to me, and listen carefully," Master Duke commanded, looking at each member of the council. "We have taken your paltry tribute." He paused.

The second man pulled out an enormous gun and played with it as if it was a toy. He pointed it at first one, then another of the council members and mouthed "Bang!" Each one cringed in turn.

"We will be back in one month to accept the rest of what you owe us," Master Duke scowled. "We want twice as many trucks loaded and ready."

He looked at each of the cowering council members. "Do you understand, Maggots?"

Before Malik or any other else responded, Master Duke turned away, slammed the door open, and marched out.

The second man pointed his gun at the *obanla*. "Bang!" he said and pulled the trigger. Malik fell to the floor. Before the sound of the gunshot died, the *oyinbo* followed his leader out of the room.

The room sat in the eerie silence. After a moment, Anana screamed and rushed forward. That broke the spell, and the council erupted in chaos as people ran in from the compound.

It took a while to sort out what happened.

Malik had not been shot but fainted. The man they called Master Clint had aimed over his shoulder. They found the bullet embedded on the far wall. The council members and their staff fluttered around like decapitated poultry. Lola pulled Josephine and Marne to her and away from where the *obanla* lay on the floor.

Once Raymon realized the *obanla* had not been killed, he shooed everyone out of the meeting room. "Come back after you've eaten. I'm sure Malik will be ready to talk then."

Instead of staying in the *obanla's* compound, Lola closed her office and took Marne and Josephine across the street to the Pines Cafe. At the councilwoman's request, the hostess led them to a small room off the main dining area where they could discuss what had happened in privacy. Marne was too upset to think of eating, but like the others she ordered the special.

While they were waiting for the food no one would eat, Lola explained to her assistants that the council had been paying tribute to the *oyinbo* motorcycle gang for several years. They called it a fee to protect the Reserve against other gangs. Although the tribute was paid out of the harvest of High Valley Fields, it was about a tenth of the production of the Babapupa farms.

"At first, that didn't seem too onerous," she explained. Last year the gang had been displeased with their payment, so the Verdant Valley council had agreed to a second tribute about a month after the first. That payment was only half as much as the original payment.

"This year our harvest is down, so we agreed to pay the original amount. Not too bad," Lola said. "But now it appears the gang is asking for three times what we paid last year."

"Talé said the harvest was down. What happens if we give these people what they are asking for?" Marne asked.

"That's what the council needs to consider." Lola frowned. "We already have to tell the rest of the Reserve that we harvested less than expected. If we give the Demon Spawn — that's the name of the gang, by the way. Awful name, isn't it? If we give the Demon Spawn a double tribute, there won't be enough for all of our people. We won't just be tightening our belts, some people will be hungry, some very hungry. The young and the old will…" Lola left her thought hanging in the air.

"The council won't let people starve, will they?" Josephine said. "They wouldn't do that. Would they?"

Before Lola could reply, the waiter brought their food. When he had left, shutting the door behind him, Lola shook her head, "I don't know. I just don't know."

Marne thought of the man with the gun, Master Clint. Would he really have shot Malik and the other council members? He hadn't pointed at her, but she had been frozen in panic. What would the council do if he started shooting them for real?

The next morning Lola strode into the office of her assistants. It was a simple room crowded with the two desks. "Where is Josephine?" she asked, glancing around the small space as if her assistant might be hiding.

"She hasn't come in yet," Marne said, looking through her display. "She was quite shook up after the meeting yesterday."

A look of consternation crossed Lola's face. "We're all upset," she said. Then she softened. "I'm surprised anyone's here. Thank you for coming in yourself."

Marne nodded. She had considered resigning as Lola's assistant, but she had a great regard for her boss and could not abandon her.

"I need you to do something for me," Lola said after a long pause. "Akande is meeting with the Hunters Guild to talk about their response to the Demon Spawn. He wanted Josephine to take minutes for him. But she's not here. Will you go instead?"

Marne stared at her desk. She had worked hard not to be in the same room as the councilman unless she had to be. Obviously her boss was not aware of the tension between Marne and her own husband. Marne shook her head while trying to think of an excuse to refuse her boss.

"You can do it," Lola assured her, "and whatever else you're working on can wait. This is more important. He's leaving in a few minutes. Gather up what you need and meet him in the courtyard." She turned to go, then turned back. "And Marne, come talk to me as soon as you return. I don't feel good about what Hackett is proposing. I'll want to know everything that goes on at this meeting." With that she walked away without giving Marne any more time to respond.

Marne saw Akande smile as he watched her walk out of the council quarters and into the bright sunlight of the courtyard. She had put a portable projector and a few personal things into a bag slung over her shoulder.

"My Little Bird," he said as she approached. "I've been looking for an opportunity to talk to you again and here you are." He licked his lips after giving her a lascivious look.

"Lola said you needed someone to take minutes and Josephine didn't come in today," Marne said dropping her eyes to a spot on the ground in front of him.

"Well, it's my lucky day, then," Akande said. He pulled her forward. When she was alongside him, he placed his hand into the small of her back.

They walked out of the *obanla's* compound and around the corner. Ahead was a two-block park modeled after the market in the capital city of Scarlet Dawn. During the summer season, the area would be full of the booths selling trinkets to visitors and supplies for villagers. Now, however, it was empty in preparation for the winter rituals honoring the Orisha. The condors, the poorest of the poor who often hung around the square, were missing.

Akande led Marne to a park bench in the center of the deserted green. He sat and pulled her down beside him. They were so close she felt his body heat and smelled his faint musky aroma. She tried to scoot away, but he wrapped his arm around her shoulder and drew her closer still. With his other hand, he turned her head, forcing her to look into his eyes.

He traced her jawline with a touch so light it sent shivers through her. "Don't be afraid, My Little Bird," he murmured, tilting her chin. "Yes," he said. "You are so beautiful."

Before she could respond, he leaned forward as if to kiss her but instead outlined her lips with his tongue. Before she could pull away, he had moved his fingers from her shoulder to the back of her head. She was caught in his grasp. Soon his tongue had worked its way into her mouth.

His free hand slid down her neck and across the cloth of her tee shirt. Keeping his touch light, he stroked her. Pulling her shirt up, he teased her waist beads, then pushed upward. Helpless tears formed in her eyes.

When he cupped her breast, pinching the nipple, an involuntary sob escaped her.

"Um, you like that, don't you, My Little Bird." He squeezed her nipple again.

She could only whimper as tears rolled down her cheeks. She had always enjoyed playing the game of men and women with her special friend Dele, but this was different. Almost dirty.

Finally, he removed his hand, pulled her shirt back down, and drew her closer. "I know you're frightened, My Little Bird," he whispered, "but there's nothing to be afraid of." He wiped the tears from her face with his thumb, first one side, then the other. "You must let me take care of you."

She didn't reply. She was ashamed. What should she do?

He pushed her upright, separating himself from her. He dug a cloth out of his pocket and gave it to her.

"Here," he said. "Clean yourself. We have an appointment at the Hunters Guild."

She wiped her eyes and blew her nose and handed the hanky back to him.

"Keep it." He waved it away. He cupped the side of her face in his hands. "So beautiful." He frowned. "We'll talk again."

He stood up, pulled her to her feet, and led her across the park toward the Guild Hall. Marne stumbled along beside him wondering what he was proposing.

"Come in, come in," Lola said when Marne tapped on the door of her combined office and sitting room that afternoon. Marne had drafted minutes of Akande's meeting and sent them to both council members. Now she needed to report to Lola. For a moment, she wondered why the councilwoman didn't talk to Akande herself. Maybe she had, and Marne's oral report was Lola's way of monitoring her work.

The councilwoman's sitting room was about the same size as her husband's. Where Akande had a separate office, she had a large desk tucked up against the far wall. This afternoon Lola was sitting in one of the more casual seating areas. Closing the display that hung above her lap, she waved Marne into a chair.

"Get yourself something to drink if you'd like. Then come join me." Lola smiled at her assistant. "I appreciate your taking Josephine's place and helping the councilman. For some reason, none of his assistants was available."

Marne hid her discomfort at the mention of Akande by pouring herself a cup of coffee from the small counter near the doorway. After their detour in the market square, Akande had kept his arm around her waist while they walked to the Guild Hall. During the whole way, he hummed to himself while she had considered how she might escape from him. However, she didn't know how she would explain herself to Lola if she didn't fulfill her assignment. Louis, Akande's assistant, met them as they approached the guild door.

"Did you enjoy your walk, sir?" Louis had said, addressing the councilman but winking at Marne.

"Of course," Akande smirked. "I always find the square stimulating this time of year. Did you bring all the files we need?"

Throughout the meeting and afterward, Akande treated her as an anonymous assistant he had brought along to take minutes for him. Louis, however, continued to leer at her as though he knew what his boss had done to her on the square. She tried to do her work without squirming under his gaze.

"How did the meeting go?" Lola said as Marne sat opposite her.

Marne pulled her mind away from her problem with Akande to focus on the councilwoman and her concerns about the guild. "Their plans are still somewhat vague," she said, "as you might expect."

She explained that the Hunters wanted to act against the incursions of the Demon Spawn into the life of Verdant Valley. "Everyone said the Spawn had been stealing from us for too long. Instead of giving in to the Spawn's demands, the guild will fight back and release us from making any tribute. This year or into the future."

"And how do they propose to do that?" Lola asked, shaking her head.

Marne explained the plan. They proposed recruiting guild members from other villages, maybe even from the capital, Scarlet Dawn. Those recruits would need training, of course. They were a police force, not an army, but the Guild felt confident they could overwhelm the Spawn when they returned at the end of the month. As one member pointed out, they had only seen about a dozen gang members. With a large enough group they could overwhelm the gang. It would be straightforward. Once the Spawn saw they were willing to fight back, the guild thought, they'd turn tail and run.

"And what do they intend to use for weapons?" Lola asked, disdain creeping into her voice. "We know the Demon Spawn have guns and they seem willing to use them. At least to intimidate us."

"That was why the guild wanted to meet with Akande before they brought their plan to the full council. They want to divert village funds to buy their own weapons. They'll need the Traders Board to help with that."

"Guns? They want to buy guns?" Now Lola sounded incredulous. "Even if the money was there, which it isn't, they think they can get firearms and train their people to go to war against the Spawn? In less than a month?"

"They propose training other villagers, too," Marne said. "Not with the guns but, they said, for more close-in combat. In case not all the Spawn run away. They think others could finish what the guild starts."

Lola looked at her, speechless. She swallowed. "The guild thinks they can train their own people, who have never handled a gun before, to intimidate and maybe kill the Demon Spawn? Then they think farmers with machetes and farm tools can mop up for them? That's their plan?"

Marne nodded. The proposal had sounded workable when Hackett described it. Now, under Lola's questioning, it appeared foolhardy, even suicidal.

Lola stared at a spot beyond Marne's shoulder for a long time. Then she stood. "Thank you for covering for Josephine and for your report," she said. "You've given me a lot to consider before the next council meeting."

Dismissed, Marne returned to the coffee counter, rinsed out her cup, and put it away. Without looking back, she left Lola alone with her thoughts about the Demon Spawn and the future of Verdant Valley.

Instead of going to her office, she started down the hallway toward the offices of the *obanla*. Perhaps Anana would have time for a break. She needed to talk. But before she took more than a couple of steps, she felt a hand sweep down her lower back and across her buttocks.

She spun around and came face-to-face with Akande.

He kissed her on the nose, whispered, "My Little Bird."

Marne stood frozen, watching him saunter away. Changing her mind about talking to Anana, she returned to her own office. She shut the door, sat down and dropped her head into her hands. She could not tell anyone about what Akande had done. Not if she wanted to keep her job. What had she gotten herself into?

CHAPTER 5

"They want what?" Halima, the Market Board's *baala*, usually stood near the entrance to the meeting hall ready to let members in and out as the meetings progressed. Today, however, Marne had watched her move into the aisle that ran from the back of the room to the center of the circle.

Lola was explaining the Demon Spawn's ultimatum. Yesterday the Verdant Valley Council had met throughout the afternoon and into the evening, trying to find a way around the demands. There were other smaller farming communities. They might call on them for help but no one else had a better harvest. Getting this new tribute from outside the valley was only robbing from the hen to feed the rooster. It would not keep starvation away from the people of the Reserve. Finally, the council turned the whole sticky mess over to the Market Board hoping their members could manufacture added stores out of thin air.

"That's what they said. We know the Spawn took this year's offering. Talé's people helped them hitch up the trailers. When they come back in a month, they expect us to have twice as many loaded and ready for them."

"Or, or…" Halima's voice trailed off.

"Clint, the one with the tattoo…" Lola looked around. Most of the people nodded. They knew Clint and his demon tattoo. "Clint shot at Malik." The room gasped. Most of them hadn't yet heard the entire story.

"Is it, is he…?" voices murmured.

"Malik wasn't hurt," Lola reassured them. "I don't think Clint meant to shoot him. Only scare him — and us." She sighed. "And it worked. The council wants us to figure out how to meet their demands."

"We can't."

"We won't."

Indignant voices bounced around the hall.

Lola pounded her walking stick, the symbol of her power as the head of the board, on the floor. The people quieted.

"Talé," she said, "tell everyone what you told me."

Talé stood. Today she was wearing work pants and a long-sleeved tee. "It's been a hard couple of years," she said. "There has been drought everywhere. Up here, down in the Republic, even over in Washatonia. I told Lola earlier that times would be hard with the regular tribute. Everyone, here and throughout the Reserve, would have to tighten our belts, especially if we want to have food for our summer visitors. But we could survive it. As I said then, nobody will be getting fat, but no one will starve either."

A relieved sigh floated over the room. Marne didn't join them. She knew Talé wasn't finished yet.

"But," Talé continued, "if we have to find twice as much as we've already given them, well…" She paused as if reluctant to continue. "Well, there's no way we can absorb that level of loss. There won't be enough food to last until the early harvest — and nothing for our visitors. I'm afraid you're looking at a downward spiral. One we can't recover from."

None of the members spoke as each person tried to assimilate Talé's report in his or her own way.

"What about getting help from the other communities?" a soft voice asked.

"I considered that back when I knew we could only offer the original quantity." Talé frowned. "We got help last year when the Spawn demanded more. I've contacted my counterparts at the other farms. We have a known amount of produce harvested. Taking the payment from somewhere else doesn't change the total needed. Whether it comes from us or it comes from elsewhere, or a combination, there isn't enough pay off the gang and feed our people. If we do this, a great number of people won't survive the winter. It's as simple as that."

Talé sat. There was nothing else to say.

Lola stood up again. "The Hunters Guild proposed another option. They will back us up. They don't think there are that many Demon Spawn. The Guild thinks we could overpower them and get them off our backs forever."

"Yes."

"Yes, of course."

"We should fight!"

Hope sounded through the hall.

"The Guild wants to put together a militia to fight the Spawn. They think if we fight back, the gang will leave us alone." Lola gauged the response of the Board members. Several were nodding with enthusiasm. "They admit there are many unknowns. We don't know, for example, how many of them there are. We do know quite a few arrive to drive away the trailers. The council thinks they're a small group trying to profit from our work. They think the gang is selling our food on the black market. If we resist, will they leave us alone or unleash the full force of their gang on us and perhaps the entire Reserve? No one knows, but the Hunters are working up a battle plan."

"We should defend ourselves," Halima said. Heads nodded.

"They have exploited us too long," another woman said.

"It's time to strike back," still another voice called out.

Caught up in the emotions of the crowd Marne didn't notice the tingling and lightheartedness she often felt out at the shrine, the feelings that often preceded a possession event. She felt herself pulling back and watching the discussion as if from a distance. As she watched, a crimson light flowed through the room coloring everyone and everything vermilion. The light liquefied and formed bloody puddles around the women's feet. Marne lifted her legs and sat cross-legged on her chair. The longer the people talked and the louder they yelled, the deeper the puddles became until they covered everyone's feet in the viscous liquid. Soon it splashed around their calves as they stood to talk or paced around. When the coppery smell became overwhelming, Marne released her hold and fell into oblivion.

Marne's eyes snapped open as blood-fear receded. A head appeared to float above her. Where was she? What happened?

"Good. You're back." The head resolved into the face of her granny. "Do you want something to drink?" She touched Marne's cheek.

As Marne sat up, she remembered. She had been in the back of the board meeting and... and.... The vision returned, vague now, like a morning dream, but the fear of it still clenched her stomach.

Granny held a cup to her lips and she sipped, surprised it wasn't the herbal concoction they always gave her after she had danced for Yemaya. Where was she?

"I saw.... I saw blood everywhere." She had to say it fast before she became overwhelmed again.

"Take more water," her granny said. "Then you can tell us about it."

As the vision receded and her head cleared, Marne realized she wasn't at the shrine, but in one of the small meeting rooms in the Board Hall. She was lying on a sofa across from a small table and chairs. Even though she thought it was still daytime outside, someone had pulled the window covering closed, leaving the room in a kind of twilight. She looked at the others surrounding her. Granny and Lola were there, as was Jumoke, her godmother, and Talé from High Valley. Halima, the *baala*, stood guard at the door as though this was some type of meeting. Where was everyone else?

Halima opened the door and Marne could hear the concern in the voices outside. The other people must still be in the big meeting room. "She's fine," Marne heard Halima say as she stepped out of the room. "Lola said we will take a recess now. Come back after lunch." When she shut the door, the voices turned into faint murmurs.

Jumoke brought a chair to sit opposite Marne. She took Marne's hands in her own. "Can you tell us what you saw, dear?"

Marne nodded, then described the vision of blood filling the meeting room.

"When did this start?" Jumoke asked, her voice soft but firm.

"I'm not sure," Marne said, trying to remember what had happened to her. "I was fine listening to Talé's report. Then Halima said something about fighting back. Yes, that's when it started." She nodded as the things clarified in her mind. "Then, everyone was talking at once, talking about fighting, hurting people. That's when I saw blood on the floor, more and more blood until it was a flood, splashing up everyone's legs." She pulled her hands away from Jumoke so she could cover her eyes and bury her face in her hands. "It was awful," she whispered.

"There, there, dear," Jumoke scooted her chair around and caressed Marne's hair. When the girl sat back up, Jumoke put her arm around her shoulders. "It's gone now. You're here with us. We'll protect you."

"No," Marne said, sure now of what she had seen. "If we fight, no one will protect us."

When the Board reconvened, Lola made Marne tell her vision to tell everyone. Some questioned why they should listen to her. She was only a young girl, barely an apprentice. Jumoke spoke for her. She told them that Marne had danced for Yemaya and been accepted her as a speaker.

"We should consider what she saw," Jumoke said. "Perhaps the Orisha have sent us a warning."

Again the meeting broke out in chaos, everyone speaking at once. Marne sat passively while Lola regained control of the meeting and the members discuss their options.

But what options did they have? They could capitulate to the Demon Spawn's demands and find enough food. Then they would watch their families, and families throughout the Reserve, starve over the winter. Someone proposed sending some families to Phoenix City, the capital of the Republic, for the winter season.

"People are starving in Phoenix," one woman said and several others agreed with her. Many of the women, like Lola, were married to members of the Traders Board. The stories the traders brought back from their trips into the Republic were horrific.

"Our people have no connections there," someone said. "They'd be lower than the condors. At least we try to take care of our poorest people. In the Republic no one cares if you're starving."

Then the talk returned to the idea of setting up a militia and attacking the gang when they returned. Marne wrapped her arms around her waist and rocked in her chair to keep herself from slipping away into another vision. Some people thought they might be able to counterattack. "At least it would give us a chance," someone said. But Marne's vision hung in the air like a veil, curbing the enthusiasm of even the most belligerent.

Finally, Talé stood. "So," she forced the group to listen, "our choice is getting killed in a bloodbath or dying from starvation." She let them consider the stark reality of the situation. "That doesn't seem like much of a choice to me. We need to find a third way, a way not based on violence." She paused again as if considering what they should do. "We're chasing our tails here. We should adjourn and go back to our families. We can meet again later after we've considered other options. There's always a third way." After looking around, she sat.

With that, Lola closed the meeting and the people silently filed out. Talé was right but where would they find her third way? Marne released the hold she'd had on herself. They would find another way, she told herself. They had to.

The next day Lola led Marne into the *obanla's* official sitting room. When Raymon, Malik's *baala*, tried to follow, she turned on him.

"I'm requesting a private meeting with Malik," she growled.

The man looked toward the *obanla*, who gave a slight nod of his head. Raymon backed away and left. Marne had been Lola's assistant long enough to know the *baala* was standing just on the other side of the door, not only keeping anyone else from entering but also eavesdropping on the conversation. Surely Malik knew he never had a private meeting.

Inside, he waved Marne and Lola to a seating area while he brought over a coffee pot and three cups on a woven tray. After he poured each of them a cup of coffee, he sat down himself.

Taking a sip, he turned to Lola. "Now, what is it you want to talk about?" His tone was mild, almost conciliatory, but Marne detected an undertone of annoyance.

"What are you planning on doing about this demand from the Spawn?" Lola stated her purpose with none of the niceties common in conversations between council members. "You know what they demand will destroy us and possibly the entire Reserve."

"We can't give them as much as they demand," Malik began. "I've been talking to other members of the council. We will offer a smaller compromise amount. I don't think they'll go for it, however. So Hackett, the head of the Hunters Guild, is right. We should be prepared to mount a defense. He's recruiting and train people." He sat back in his chair and took another sip of his coffee. "I've been in contact with the *obanla* in Scarlet

Dawn. He has promised to send members of his own Hunters Guild and to rally guilds from the other villages. By the end of the month, we should have a strong force to defend ourselves against the Spawn."

"And what will you be using as weapons?" Lola asked.

"We'll have to acquire guns, of course," Malik said.

"You're planning on recruiting, arming, and training a militia to go against an armed gang of who-knows-how-many experienced and desperate men. In one month," Lola asked, sarcasm dripping from her wide lips.

Malik smiled. "Exactly. Hackett doesn't think the gang is much bigger than we've seen. Ten, twelve men at most. He is positive he can have an overpowering force ready by the time the Spawn returns."

"I see you have it all worked out." Lola leaned back and sipped her coffee.

Marne was amazed at Lola's brazen attitude toward the man who was their high ruler. The woman appeared fearless.

After a long silence, Lola leaned forward again. "And you have confirmed the wisdom of this with your chief diviner and Orula, the Orisha of divination? Has the Guild confirmed this plan with its patrons, Ogun, the owner of all weapons, and Ochosi, the voice of justice? I assume you have their support for this plan?"

As Lola talked, Malik sank deeper into his chair until at the end he looked like a little boy enduring a tongue-lashing from one of his aunts. It was obvious that they had not talked to the deities who would be expected to give support and spiritual aid.

"N-no," Malik stuttered. "There hasn't been time." He sat straighter as if aware of his position. "But we will. I'm sure the Orisha will support us in this. They don't want us to starve. They don't want the collapse of the Reserve."

"My market women haven't had a chance to talk to the Orisha either," Lola said.

A flash of contempt crossed the *obanla's* face as if to say, "See, you are no better than we are."

"But," she continued, "they have spoken to us." She glared at him until he looked away.

When he set his cup back on the table, Lola turned to Marne. "I don't know if you remember Marne Abelabu, my new assistant."

He frowned, apparently confused about where this conversation was going. But Marne knew. She was here to represent the voice of Yemaya, the Mother of All. She nodded to Malik.

"Marne has just been confirmed as a speaker for Yemaya. She has been working for me in my shop and will join Gladys out at her workshop. And she's a member of my board."

Lola looked back at Malik. "Marne, tell *Malik* what you saw at our board meeting."

Marne swallowed hard. She had never expected her vision would be taken to the *obanla*. "Lola was telling the board about the gang's demands," she began. "When she talked about the Guild fighting back, the hall seemed to fill with red light. Then, then…" Caught in the memory of her vision, Marne continued, ending with "Blood, blood. There was blood everywhere." Again she buried her head in her hands, the horror alive again in her mind.

Malik sipped his coffee. "You're a new speaker, are you not?"

Marne looked at him. "Yes, sir. Yemaya said I should be her speaker when I was initiated, but I wasn't confirmed until two weeks ago."

"Well, as you mature in your role as a speaker, you'll realize that not everything you see is a vision. And that sometimes visions are difficult to interpret." He leaned back. "How do you know all that blood was our blood and not the blood of the Demon Spawn?"

"I-I," she stuttered. She had never considered that. "I just do," she said.

"You don't know, not really," the *obanla* said, his voice dripping with disdain. "You were overwrought by these circumstances. Yours is only one interpretation." He turned to Lola. "As you suggest, we'll confirm our plan with Orula and I expect the Guild will confirm their part with Ogun and Ochosi."

Then he turned back to Marne, "In the meantime, my dear, you don't need to worry about this. The council and Hunters have it well under control." He reached out and patted Marne's knee. "Spend more time out at your shrine, learning the speaker's craft, instead of worrying about things are beyond your understanding."

When he stood up, Lola and Marne did likewise.

"Lola," he said. "I expect you to support the council's decision. If you can't do that, I'll ask that the Market Board appoint a new representative." He opened the door to the council offices. When Lola and Marne stood in the hallway, he said, "Do I make myself clear?" He slammed the door shut without waiting for an answer.

CHAPTER 6

Lola took Marne out to her granny's workshop after their meeting with the *obanla*. Lola said, "I need to talk to someone and Gladys is always so clear-headed."

Now they were in her granny's cozy sitting room. Two of the walls were covered with lengths of Gladys's famous indigo cloth. There were several groups of chairs and tables scattered around. The older women sat together on the sofa staring into their glasses of beer, while Marne took a chair set at an angle to them, with a mug of tea.

"So, what are you going to do?" Granny asked when Lola described the *obanla's* response to Marne's retelling of her vision.

"I don't know," Lola said. "There's nothing I can do. Wherever I look I see is death and destruction. Either the slow death by starvation or the instant annihilation of a war with the Demon Spawn. Malik has convinced the Hunters Guild that they can win in a battle against guns." She shook her head. "Even if we could get enough weapons, which we can't, our people don't know how to use them — especially against someone who is shooting back." She stopped. Her eyes were unfocused, staring into a future she couldn't accept and didn't know how to change.

Granny put her arm around Lola's shoulder and patted her knee. "There, there, dear, we'll think of something. We'll find another way to meet this challenge."

The women sat in silence. Their beer got warm while Marne's tea cooled.

Then her granny sang something that Marne didn't recognize, keeping her rhythm by tapping the heel of her foot on the floor. After the third or fourth time, as her granny's voice become louder and louder, Marne heard the words. They made little sense to her. "*Pinkun! Pinkun! Ajanbiti!*" Granny chanted. "*Pinkun! Pinkun! Ajanbiti!*"

Marne watched Lola's face. Fear chased away despair with a hint of defiance.

"No." Lola frowned. "No, I won't."

"*Pinkun! Pinkun! Ajanbiti!*" Marne's granny continued, adding, "We are *Iyami*, we are the mothers. *Pinkun! Pinkun! Ajanbiti!* We are *Iyami*, we are the mothers."

"I will not." Lola answered some unspoken question in Granny's voice. "I am not a witch and I will not."

Marne remembered an afternoon during her first menstrual cycle. Her granny and a group of older women came to her father's apartment to proclaim her a woman and put on her waist beads. She had received her *omodo*, the smooth wooden club that was the tool of the *Iyami*, on that day, too. The women told her then the secret of the *Iyami*, the witches. Even children knew they were powerful beings that met, it was said, to make trouble. Few people called them by their name, preferring to refer to them as the *Iyami*, our mothers, as though they were loving and benevolent.

"This is a something all women know," Granny told her that day. "We are the witches. All women carry the *aje*, the witch substance, in our bellies. Our witch substance is the power of life, and the power of death."

Now, Marne realized, Granny was singing the rallying cry of the *Iyami*. Would the women in front of her change into grotesque versions of themselves to wreck vengeance on the people of Verdant Valley, in full daylight?

Lola swung her head back and forth like a speaker trying to refuse the call of an Orisha. "No," she moaned. "I will not."

Marne's granny took her arm from around Lola's shoulders and held her hands, refusing to let her escape her words. "*Pinkun! Pinkun! Ajanbiti! We are Iyami*, we are the mothers."

Lola continued to writhe, ducking and fighting as though trying to avoid invisible blows.

After a few minutes, Granny chanted softer and softer until only an echo remained.

As the room fell into silence, Lola quieted. Marne recognized that liminal state after a possession event when the spirit had departed but the speaker was not yet fully in her body.

Marne stood up and collected the half-full beer glasses and her teacup, neglected and cold. In a moment she returned with a bowl of cool water and a clean rag. Using both hands, in the ritual manner, she presented the bowl to her granny who accepted it in the same way.

Back in the kitchen she put a glass of water on a tray for each of them, along with fresh glasses of beer for Lola and her granny.

When she returned to the sitting room, Lola was herself again, although somewhat dazed by the experience. Marne set the tray on the table between herself and the other women.

Holding her water glass up in salute, Granny nodded to Lola and Marne encouraging them to do likewise. "We are *Iyami*, we are the mothers." They raised their glasses and touched them to Granny's glass. "We are *Iyami*, we are the mothers."

Something had changed among them, although Marne didn't know what it was. She had been initiated into a ritual of womanhood without any understanding of what that meant.

Finishing the water, Lola set her glass back on the tray. "You're right." Her voice was stronger than it had been since she and Marne had left Malik's compound. "I can't, we can't allow this thing." Her eyes brightened and her spine straightened. "If I have to march, if we have to march to the *obanla's* compound naked, in the middle of the day, we must prevent this disaster."

"*Ashé O*," Granny said, setting her own glass on the table and gripping Lola's hands in her own. "I am with you, Sister. We are all with you."

Marne stared at the two women. Both had changed from an attitude of hopelessness to something else. They looked defiant, as though through the power of the *Iyami* they could change what was happening between Verdant Valley and the Demon Spawn. And, perhaps they could.

The following day Marne and Granny were working alone in the workshop. There would be a tea party for a group of women later, but for the moment the two of them were pretending life was continuing. As Granny's principal apprentice, Marne was helping to sort out her patterns. She looked at the new ones her granny had developed over the summer season when it was too hot to work with the dye pots. Granny promised to allow Marne to transfer the simpler designs to the test cloths to calibrate the dye.

Without looking up, Granny asked, "So did you find any likely young men this summer?"

Marne was caught by surprise. She was sixteen years old, mature enough to explore the ways of men and women and her future as a wife and mother. She had enjoyed flirting and playing with the older boys and unmarried men who hung around the Market during the long summer days. Not that Lola permitted her to idle away her time. Her boss wanted her working, serving customers, and doing the other chores associated with a retail business. Now that the shop had closed and she was at the *obanla* compound, there was even less chance to flirt and play.

"No one in particular," she said, "although…" She faltered, embarrassed. Late in the summer she had spent much of her free time with Dele, one of those who were always hanging around the Market. He was ten years older than Marne and seemed so sophisticated and mature. He had introduced her to many of the ways men and women came together. But she wasn't sure she wanted to discuss that with Granny.

"Well, don't be in too big of a hurry," her granny said. "Harrumph. Those boys are not your only options. Most of the good men are too busy to be hanging around all day." She turned to pick up an older pattern. "I should talk to your father," she mumbled. "That man spends all of his time thinking about himself and forgets about you girls."

Marne brushed her waist beads through the thin material of her tee shirt. She loved the quietly audible clicking noises they made. Would her father look for a husband for her? Other girls her age were getting marriage offers. She smiled to herself. Maybe Dele would come for her.

"How is your friend Anana doing?" her granny asked in an abrupt change of topic. "I haven't seen that baby of hers recently."

Marne was surprised Granny had taken an interest in her friend and her child. Her granny who was all barbs and harsh words toward her apprentices melted when she saw Anana and her son Karamat. Whenever her granny came by to see Marne and her sister Perla, she always made a point of stopping by Anana's apartment.

"She went back to work a couple months ago," Marne said. "One of the other wives takes care of her son during the day. Did you know she's one of the *obanla's* assistants?"

"Bad timing, I'd say," Granny snorted. "She should petition for more maternity leave."

"Oh, no. She had more time, but she was eager to go return. She was in line for a promotion when Kara was born and she didn't want someone else to beat her to it."

"So she likes working for Malik?" Granny asked, looking up.

Marne nodded. "Yes. She loves the work."

"What about that Spawn who stayed behind when the others left? The one who shadows the *obanla* everywhere? Doesn't he scare her?"

"Everyone's scared of Master Clint. He's always around, leering at us and smirking. We're afraid we might find ourselves alone with him." Marne's voice trailed off. She didn't want to upset her granny or make her worry about Marne's other job. But the Spawn enforcer had commented on their looks, rating them and implying he wanted to do more than just watch them work. Anana had become a special focus of his attention and he'd called her "Tits," much to everyone's discomfort.

"I heard one carries a weapon," Granny said.

Marne nodded. "He's the one who shot at Malik that first day. He comes to meetings wearing those bandoliers full of bullets crisscrossing his chest and playing with that gun." She shivered. "I don't know how the council members can even do their work."

Granny cocked her eyebrow in a question.

"He likes to point his gun at whoever is speaking," Marne explained. "If he doesn't like what they're saying, he says 'bang' just loud enough that everyone hears. We're afraid he might shoot at someone else, but he hasn't, not yet at least."

Throwing the final patterns into a basket, her granny stood up. "That's sufficient for today," she said. "Why don't you bring Anana by tomorrow night for tea?"

Marne nodded. Her friend liked Granny and would feel honored to be invited to one of her parties.

"Come in, come in," Marne's granny greeted Marne and Anana when they knocked on the door to her home the following evening. Unlike almost everyone else in the Reserve, Granny didn't live in a family compound but in a small building attached to her workshop. After her only child, Marne's mother, died, she no longer felt welcome in her husband's compound. Nor, she told her granddaughters, was she comfortable in her own family's compound.

"I left when I was about your age," she said. So she had built a cozy little house in the one place where she felt at home, her own workshop. Many times Marne had wished her granny had a larger house. After her mother died, Marne wanted to escape from her compound, her inattentive father, and his demanding new wife. She dreamed of joining her granny but there was no room for her there. Besides, soon she would find the right young man to marry. Then she would move into his compound and begin her own life.

In the meantime, Marne enjoyed visiting Granny, especially during the breaks between the summer visitor season and winter when the dye pots demanded her granny's attention.

Today Granny had invited Marne for an evening visit. At first Marne thought her granny wanted to talk about the commotion she had caused at the Market Board meeting or her upcoming stint as an apprentice. But then she had told Marne to bring Anana, too.

Marne wondered whether they should have brought Kara along but, as they walked into her granny's sitting room, Marne again suspected this wasn't just a friendly visit. Lola, Jumoke, and Talé, some of the most influential of the market women, were waiting for them. Marne questioned her granny with her eyes. But Granny only smiled and pointed them toward the sitting room.

"Welcome, Marne, Anana. I'm glad you could make it." She glanced around. "You know everyone, don't you, Anana?"

Marne's friend nodded, her open face clouded with suspicion. Lola didn't seem to notice the girl's unease.

"Did Marne explain to you want happened?" Again Lola addressed Anana.

Marne's vision was not a secret. All market women knew what she had seen. No one had said not to tell anyone else. Anana seemed wary of where Lola was going.

"Did you share what you heard from Marne with Malik?"

Anana looked like a startled deer. She shook her head.

"It's not important if you had," Lola said. "I've talked to him and to the rest of the council. In private, not at a meeting."

Relief flooded Anana's face.

"Do you want to know what they told me?"

The girls glanced at each other and then nodded in unison.

"The board members were concerned, but the *obanla* discounted Marne's vision as the hysterics of a girl who'd just put on waist beads. They think our people can defeat Spawn. And they're not worried about any losses we might suffer." Lola frowned and glanced at the other women. "Can you believe that?"

The others shook their heads, frowning.

"What do you think, Anana?" Lola asked. "You've been working for Malik for how many years now?"

"Four," Anana whispered.

"What do you think, based on your experience?"

Marne sensed a trap and guessed that Anana did too, but there was nothing for her to do but respond.

"Marne told me what happened." Anana's voice barely audible in the quiet room. "She said you were looking for a third way. Something that didn't depend on fighting."

"Good girl," Lola smiled. "You've caught us up and cut to the heart of the problem. That's why we're here. We're searching for a solution based on working together, not conflict."

Jumoke spoke up then. "We, these women here, think we can find another way out of this crisis. You're smart and you know how the council works. We'd appreciate your help. We want you to join our sisterhood, the Sisterhood of Moon, since we have one month to develop a plan." She paused. "Will you join us?"

After a moment of silence, Marne's granny began singing under her breath. When the other women joined her, Marne recognized the *Iyami* chant, "*Pinkun! Pinkun! Ajanbiti!* We are *Iyami*, we are the mothers. *Pinkun! Pinkun! Ajanbiti!* We are *Iyami*, we are the mothers."

Marne watched fear, hope, and then something like pleasure roll across Anana's face.

When the song ebbed toward silence, Anana nodded. "I can't betray Malik," she said.

"Of course not," Lola agreed. "We wouldn't ask that of you."

"Then, yes, if I can help save Verdant Valley and Babapupa, I'll become a member of your sisterhood." She looked at the women, who returned her smile.

Marne glanced around. Five women had formed a sisterhood to find the third way. Five was a good number, the number of the Orisha Oshun. As a goddess Oshun represented many parts of the world. As the young woman, vibrant and full of vitality, she and her followers enjoyed the sensual things in life. In her stories she conquered by erotic passion rather than violence. An appropriate patroness for the group.

But Marne felt left out. These were adult women who were planning on working together to find Talé's third way. As the *obanla* had said, she was just a young girl barely into her waist beads. It appeared the only thing they wanted her for was to bring Anana into their circle.

The room was silent. Then she heard her name.

"What about you?" She glanced toward the women. "We consider you a part of our sisterhood but we haven't asked you. Will you join us as well?"

Relief flooded through Marne. They didn't think she was too young. They were not leaving her out. She nodded, "Yes, yes. I want to join. I want to be in your sisterhood."

"*Ashé.*" So be it. The others stood up and pulled Marne into a hug, accepting her as a member of their sorority. Was she also one of the *Iyami*?

When everyone sat back down, Marne looked around. Now they were six, the number of Shango who represented masculine energy. The passion of fire and violence, the lightning that killed without warning. In the stories, Shango was often described as the opponent of Ogun, the patron of the Hunters Guild. Shango was usually the winner of those confrontations. Marne wondered whether the premier representation of masculinity was a good patron for a sisterhood of women who needed to succeed by guile and not force.

Marne was a speaker for Yemaya, the owner of the oceans and the waters that flowed into them. She was the Great Mother, the mother of the people of Babapupa. But also, Marne realized with a start, the mother of everyone, even the Demon Spawn. Both Oshun and Yemaya were associated with women's blood but it was Yemaya who had showed Marne the flood of blood. The sisterhood seemed unbalanced to her, teetering on the edge of Shango's double-headed ax, as likely to fall into violence as to discover Talé's third way.

We need a seventh sister, Marne thought. Someone to bring us under the protection of Yemaya. Someone with a mother's concern for villagers and the Spawn alike. Where would they find such a person?

CHAPTER 7

"Welcome to the Verdant Valley Village Council." Malik could barely say the words as the other council members cowered in their seats.

The Demon Spawn who returned the tribute trucks had not gone back to their own people as they had in past years. Instead, they rode their cycles into the village center. A handful of them joined Master Clint in his occupation of the *obanla*'s compound and the council offices. After a closed-door meeting in Malik's office, the *obanla* had called a special session of the council, attended by Master Clint and several of the Spawn.

"Duke sent us here to be sure you follow his instructions," Master Clint told them. The remaining gang members arranged themselves around the perimeter of the room. "We don't want any funny stuff."

Master Clint demanded that they provide living quarters for his people. Each council member hosted one of the Spawn while they assigned the rest of the gang to other compounds. They became a menacing presence throughout the village. They were everywhere, watching, listening, and spying on the people. They seldom interacted with the villagers, not even returning common greetings. Instead, they just glared at anyone trying to go about their business.

The Hunters Guild's plan to train and arm villagers and visiting guild members was abandoned. Marne didn't know how it happened, but all evidence of their recruiting and training efforts disappeared during that first Spawn-run council meeting. She heard there was clandestine talk of moving the sessions deep into the woods, where they might not be observed. However, as far as she knew they had stopped all their efforts. She thought the Guild was still communicating with their counterparts in the other villages and in Scarlet Dawn.

Meetings took on an oppressed air as Master Clint seized Akande's position to Malik's right. Now Malik, Akande, and the rest of the council tried to manage the business of the village, foregoing, of course, any discussion of the Demon Spawn's demands.

Carrying on was difficult since Master Clint appeared to be easily bored. He spent most of the meeting time playing with a huge knife or his gun. He kept everyone on edge by pointing his weapon at random members or whoever was speaking and mouthing "Bang." Marne and the other assistants, who sat behind their council members, feared Master Clint would again fire at members. Or as he had done earlier, he might purposely miss the council member and hit one of them.

Terrified after the Spawn's initial invasion and the shooting of Malik, Josephine resigned as Lola's assistant. Marne heard her family had sped up Josephine's wedding plan and moved her into her new husband's compound in another village. Marne was no longer Lola's assistant-in-training but simply her assistant. Despite the presence of Master Clint and the other Spawn in and out of their offices, she and Lola carried out their duties. They did not mention the Sisterhood of the Moon or Talé's third way. It appeared that resistance to the demands of the gang had collapsed.

Marne and Anana's home compound was too small and unimportant to become a billet for the Spawn, so the two young women could escape there after the work. Marne and her sister Perla cooked and cleaned as they had since their mother died four years earlier. And even though their father remarried a mere six months after their mother's funeral, his new wife continued to leave the household tasks to the girls.

The sisters often talked about how the woman whose name they refused to use spent her days in their father's private rooms. However, since he had put in a separate entrance, they seldom saw her. They knew she and their father were regularly gone into the late evenings. Occasionally, when the woman could no longer stand the sordid condition of her apartment, she opened it to let the girls try to scrub it back to a modicum of cleanliness.

Marne's job at Lola's shop and now in the *obanla's* compound changed the rhythm of the girls' days. They figured out how Marne could work for both Lola and their granny while still carrying her share of the household tasks. Perla did more of the shopping and cooking while Marne did what she could in the evenings and whenever she had a day off. But the Demon Spawn interrupted many of the winter activities of the village, including at her granny's studio.

After the first meeting of the Sisterhood, Marne's granny notified her apprentices that "due to the unusual circumstances" she would not be firing up her dye pots until "sometime later." There was no reason to open the workshop if the gang was going to force everyone to leave Babapupa or starve. Tears slipped down Marne's face when she thought of the bolts of plain cloth and the pounds of indigo that sat waiting for her grandmother and the other apprentices — cloth and dye that might never meet and produce the stunning fabric that made her granny famous throughout the Reserve and beyond.

Marne's grandmother began having small tea parties in her home. She invited different women for drinks and light conversation. As her assistant, Marne attended most of the events, spending her time passing around trays of nibbles and refilling glasses and cups.

One day, the members of Sisterhood arrived and Marne discovered that, just as Malik was being shadowed by Master Clint, Lola had her own Demon Spawn keeper.

Lola introduced Li'l Meg to the group as "my leash." The woman was not much older than Anana, but was grim-faced and angry looking. Like the other gang members, she was dressed in black, including a leather jacket, tee-shirt, trousers and heavy black work boots. She scowled as Lola introduced her.

"We call ourselves the Sisterhood of the Moon," Lola told Li'l Meg, much to Marne's surprise. She expected they would have kept the sisterhood secret from any of the Demon Spawn.

Once Marne passed around a tray of nibbles and filled the cups and glasses, Lola looked at the group. "Let's start by introducing ourselves," she said. She turned to Li'l Meg. "As you know, I am Lola. As the head of the Market Board, I am also a member of the council. I have a small shop along the main street of Verdant Valley although it is closed now for the season." She gestured to the woman sitting next to her in the circle.

"Welcome to my home," Marne's granny said. "My name is Gladys. I am a dyer of cloth. My workshop is just over there. I can give you a tour later if you'd like." She nodded to Marne.

"Greetings." Marne smiled at the Spawn woman, who glanced at her and then looked away as if ashamed of that little show of interest. "Gladys is my granny and I will be one of her apprentices when she fires up the dye pots. I am also apprenticed to Councilwoman Lola."

Li'l Meg pulled out a knife like the one Clint used to terrorize the council. She put one of her heavy boots on the opposite knee and began cleaning the soles, letting the dirt and debris drop onto the floor.

The rest of the women introduced themselves with no response or acknowledgment from their guest.

When they finished, Lola said, "Thank you, my sisters." Then she turned to Li'l Meg. When the woman refused to meet her eyes, Lola asked, "Would you introduce yourself?"

The Spawn woman changed legs so she could clean her second boot. "You know who I am and why I'm here."

Silence filled the room. Then Marne's granny began her soft chanting, "Pinkun! Pinkun! Ajanbiti!"

"Well," Talé said. "We're here to explore the third way."

Again Marne was surprised that the other women were being so open about their purpose. Then she realized that Talé was speaking in a code Li'l Meg probably didn't understand.

"Today, I want us to think about the tale of Oshun and Ogun. I'll begin by telling the story for the benefit of our guest."

Marne's granny stopped chanting. Then Lola smiled at Li'l Meg, who had not looked up from her boot-cleaning.

"Oshun and Ogun are two of our Orisha, our deities. Oshun is the most beautiful of women, young and lithesome, while Ogun is the blacksmith who works hard every day. Once, Ogun got angry with the other Orisha. He left the forge and fled into the forest. Soon the other Orisha realized that no new tools were being crafted and none of the older tools were being repaired."

Talé stopped and looked around the room ending at Li'l Meg. The Spawn woman continued to clean the bottom of her boot.

"Already, the Orisha had rejected the first way," Talé continued. "They couldn't just leave Ogun in the forest. Without Ogun to make and repair their tools, none of them could do their own work. They had to consider other options.

"So the Orisha met to discuss how they might persuade Ogun to return to the forge," Talé said. "First, the great king Obatala stepped forward. 'Ogun has always been a loyal subject,' he said. 'When I explain that we need him, he will return.' 'Yes, yes,' everyone said, 'you can convince Ogun to return.' So Obatala walked into the forest. The other Orisha waited several days until Obatala returned. It was plain by his bedraggled clothing and dejected expression he had not been successful.

"Then, Eleggua stepped forward. 'They don't call me Silver-Tongued for nothing,' he said. 'I will go into the forest.' 'Yes, yes,' everyone said, 'you can convince Ogun to return.' So off Eleggua went. The other Orisha waited several days until Eleggua returned. It was plain from his despondent walk he had not been successful.

Then, Shango stepped forward. 'Ogun is strong but I am stronger,' he said. 'I will go into the forest and convince him to return.' 'Yes, yes,' everyone said, 'you can convince Ogun to return.' So Shango sauntered off. The Orisha waited several days until Shango returned. It was plain from the tears in his clothes and the dirt on his face he and Ogun had fought but only Shango returned.

"Each Orisha stepped forward in turn, convinced that he or she could convince Ogun to return. Even the owner of the marketplace and warrior woman, Oya, volunteered. Every one returned wretched and alone."

Talé stopped her storytelling a second time. "What have we learned so far?"

The women knew the story, and what each of the Orisha represented.

"Obatala represents the power of authority," Lola said, "but he wasn't able to order Ogun to return."

"Eleggua represents the power of persuasion," Marne's granny said, "but he wasn't able to coax Ogun to return."

"Shango and Oya are both warriors," Jumoke said enjoying the story and where it was leading. "They represent the power of strength, the power of the sword. But they could not force Ogun to return."

Talé nodded smiling. Marne noticed that although Li'l Meg was still looking at the sole of her boot, she had stopped poking at it. She, too, was caught up in the tale.

"Finally," Talé continued, "Oshun, the youngest of the Orisha, stepped forward. 'I will go into the forest,' she said. 'I will coax Ogun to return.' Everyone laughed. Oshun was a delightful young woman, but she had no authority and wasn't a warrior. She was no match for Ogun, the blacksmith who had already defeated the other Orisha. Eleggua spoke up for her. 'We have all tried and failed. We should at least let Oshun try.' Still laughing, they agreed, but they were determined to follow her. To protect her, they told themselves.

"Before heading to Ogun's secret place, Oshun returned to her compound and found five of the most exquisite of her scarves. Again the Orisha who were following her laughed. 'Oshun thinks she can conquer Ogun with nothing more than flimsy scarves,' they said. When she sashayed into the forest, she didn't go to where everyone knew Ogun was. Instead she danced along, singing to herself until she came to a long lazy river. Arranging her scarves on the shrubs, she disrobed and walked into the river, still singing. By this time Oshun knew she had caught the attention of Ogun who was hiding in the bushes. As she bathed, taking special pains to caress every portion of her luscious young body, he watched, moaning. Ogun didn't even notice when Oshun, stepping naked from the water, tied his hands together with one of her gauzy scarves. She pulled him from the underbrush and draped another scarf around his neck. Then she used the remaining the scarves to tie those two scarves together to form a rope. Still singing and dancing, Oshun led the blacksmith back to his forge. As Oshun untied the scarves from Ogun and wrapped them around her still-naked body, he shook himself as though awaking from a dream."

Talé looked over to Marne, the youngest of the gathered women.

Marne nodded. "Oshun the Beautiful didn't have to force Ogun out of the forest," she said, picking up the story. "She used a third way, and he followed her willingly. She led him to where the other Orisha were waiting. They made a feast to welcome him back among their company."

Talé laughed and clapped her hands together, nodding as though Marne had said something brilliant. Soon the other women were laughing and clapping. Marne basked in their admiration, even though every one of the women, everyone in Verdant Valley, everyone in the Reserve knew the story. They had heard it hundreds of times. It was a special favorite of those like Talé who were the worshippers of Oshun.

When the sisterhood talked of finding a third way to cope with the Demon Spawn, Marne had not thought of this story. However, it was a perfect example of what they were trying to achieve. Bathing naked in the river and dancing through the forest would not convince the gang to leave without their added tribute. But Marne and the other women understood the principle. They needed to find a similarly unique solution to their problem.

Li'l Meg dropped her booted foot, crushing the dirt she'd removed and working it into what had been a clean floor. "I don't get it," she snarled, drawing everyone's attention from Marne.

The laugher died away although the smiles remained. Talé nodded. "I know." She smiled. "I know you don't."

CHAPTER 8

"Where's Lola?" It was late the following afternoon when Akande burst into Marne's workspace. "She's not in her office."

"Iya Lola's gone with Malik to meet with Talé and some other farmers. I don't think she'll be back today, but I can tell her you were looking for her." Marne tried to maintain a cordial and competent manner. He was, after all, an important councilman and her boss's husband.

His smile was all teeth, like a wolf's. "Come with me. I need your help."

Marne looked around as though there were someone else he could be talking to, but she was alone.

"Lola won't even know," he said as if to reassure her. "Besides, we have to work together in these treacherous times. Don't we, My Little Bird?"

Marne shook her head, wanting to deny him. He stood with the door ajar, waiting for her. She wondered what he needed from her that one of his own assistants could not do.

"Come along now," he demanded, turning and walking away.

Confused, Marne followed him. The lights in his sitting room were dimmed except for a single small lamp. Louis was there pouring wine into two glasses on a table in front of the sofa where she and Akande sat together on her earlier visit.

"Thank you, Louis," Akande said. "Please see that I am not disturbed — by anyone."

Marne heard the ominous click of the door locking behind Akande's assistant.

He relaxed on the couch and patted the seat next to him. Someone had removed the chairs that would normally be part of this seating area, so she had no choice.

She perched as far from him as she could. He picked up the two glasses, handed her one, and then scooted so close that their shoulders, hips, and legs touched, his faint musky aroma enveloping her. He held up his glass in a salute and waited until she responded, touching her goblet to his. "To our future." He held half the liquid for a moment before swallowing.

"You remember what I told you about drinking?" he asked.

She nodded. Then as he watched, she filled her mouth, held it, and swallowed.

"Good girl," he nodded. "I knew you remembered."

He emptied his glass. "Your turn." He set it on the table.

She took another mouthful, held it, and swallowed again. This time the wine was summer sunshine filling her belly. Despite her discomfort being alone with Akande, she relaxed.

He removed her goblet from her hand and set it next to his.

Turning back to her, he cupped the side of her face in his hand. "Do you know how beautiful you are, My Little Bird?"

She stared into his eyes, afraid of what he planned do to her in this locked room. She knew most of the staff had left for the day and Louis was standing outside to prevent her escape.

He slid his palm around the back of her head and pulled it toward his own. She tasted the wine on his lips, and then on his tongue as it pushed its way into her mouth.

With his other hand, he traced the curve of her ear, her jaw line, and the curve of her neck. He pushed under her blouse, laying his palm on her chest. While his fingers were exploring the bare skin above the swell of her breast, his tongue pulled back. Then, after nipping her lower lip, he drew it into his mouth.

He unbuttoned first his own shirt, then hers. After placing her hand against his chest so she cupped his muscle, he placed his own palm on her exposed breast. She whimpered when he pinched her nipple, bringing it to attention.

Without deciding to do so, she followed his lead as he massaged and squeezed first one breast, then the other. He moaned responding to her touch.

When he dropped his hand and stroked her belly, she mirrored his actions. As she rubbed his stomach, he pushed her palm onto the bulge of his penis.

"Oh, My Little Bird," he sighed, dropping his head. When he drew her nipple between his lips, she gasped, and whimpered. Soon Marne was lost in the caress of Akande's mouth and hands on her body along with the feel his manhood under her palm.

Over the summer she had engaged in sexual games with those flirty young boys hanging around the market. Dele and others taught her so much. However, none of them inflamed her the way this older man did.

Floating on the bliss of her feelings, Marne heard the locked door click open.

"Sir," Louis stepped into the room.

She groaned as Akande pulled away from her breast and tugged the edges of her shirt over her nipples.

"What?" he said. "I told you I didn't want to be interrupted."

"I'm sorry, sir," Louis started. "Master Clint…"

"Out of the way, Scum." As Clint's voice moved into the room, Marne froze. She forgot to pull her blouse closed or to button it.

Marne watched Akande's expression changed from dreamy pleasure to anger. Suddenly, he was the politician, smiling in welcome.

"Master Clint," Akande said, standing up and moving toward the entrance. He did not try to dress himself, leaving his shirt unbuttoned, his sleek brown chest exposed. "Did we have an appointment?"

"I don't need appointments and I don't like locks," Clint snarled. "I don't want to find any more closed doors, get it?"

"Yes, sir," Akande stammered, his usual smooth persona ruffled. "My offices are always open to you."

Then Clint must have noticed Marne on the sofa in the soft light of the lamp. "Oh, I see you were entertaining." Clint's voice softened. "What are you doing here, darling?"

Her blouse was closed but remained unbuttoned. She knew she looked disheveled, like a girl who had been doing what she was doing.

Clint's lecherous tone galvanized Marne who fumbled with her shirt, finally getting it buttoned. There was nothing she could do about her hair or her aroused look. Then, without warning, the Demon Spawn was across the room and sitting next to her. She tried to push herself farther away but was stopped by the armrest.

He wasn't a big man but was powerfully built. Sometime during the day he had removed the bandoliers and black leather jacket. Now he wore a leather vest over a sleeveless white tee-shirt. His muscular arms were well-defined, accentuated by the fiendish tattoo of a brilliant red dragon slithering up to his right shoulder. He smelled of dust, the desert, and unbridled manhood. The gun he used against Malik hung in its holster on his hip, dark and menacing.

"You didn't have to dress for me, darling," he murmured, cupping her breast for a moment. He looked to where Akande and Louis still stood in the shadows. "We should make Malik the Milquetoast add this one to our tribute."

Marne cringed at his touch. She glanced toward where she thought the councilman was watching. Her eyes begged him to help. But he remained silent as Clint unbuttoned her shirt and pulled it aside.

"Ah, luscious. So young and fresh." Clint fondled her breasts, kneading and pinching them, his calloused fingertips exciting her against her will.

Marne whimpered, a tear rolling down her cheek.

"Yes," Clint said, ignoring her reaction to his touch. "I need to spend more time with you, darling." Again he looked toward the shadows. "You'll share her with me, won't you, my friend?"

Akande remained silent. Then he said, "Did you want to talk to me?"

"Of course." Clint gave Marne a last salacious look, dragging his index finger between her breasts, down her belly, and across her waist beads. Retracing his path, he moved his hand until it again encircled her breast. Tugging the nipple between his lips, he sucked, then released it with a sharp nip. She gasped. He carefully buttoned her shirt. "Do you work for my friend, Akande?"

"N-no, sir," she mumbled. "I'm Iya Lola's assistant."

"Well," he drew out his words, "you tell your Iya Lola that you'll being 'working' for me now." He licked his lips and winked at her. Then he leaned back and waved his hand, dismissing her. "I'll come find you, don't you worry."

Marne stood up and crept to the doorway, slipping past Akande who was still standing in the shadows. When she got out into the hallway, Louis grabbed her. "Tell no one you've been here," he hissed. "Do you understand?"

Marne felt like a fly caught in a spider's web, tears streaming down her face.

"Do you understand?" Louis asked again, squeezing her arm.

When Marne nodded, he released her.

She stumbled back into her office. She closed the door and leaned against it. What had she done? How could she face Anana and the other assistants? Lola? What would she tell Lola? Where could she go? What could she do? How could she escape the disgrace of being discovered with Lola's husband? She shuddered. Perhaps she could hide from Lola and Akande — he hadn't yet revealed their secret meetings — but how was she going to avoid Master Clint and the other Demon Spawn? She could still feel Clint's hands scraping against the delicate skin of her breasts, his bite, his salacious touch raking her body. Her shirt seemed to emanate a mixture of Akande's musk and Clint's dusty desert scent.

She held her breath as someone walked past her office. When the hallway was silent again, she turned out the light. Anyone else passing by would think she had left.

In her darkened office she fell into her chair and wept, burying her face in her hands so no sound escaped.

The next day Marne was awakened by Perla pounding on her sleeping room door. "Wake up, sleepyhead," she called. "You will be late to work."

Marne sat up and then lay back when the soft fabric of her nightshirt rubbed against her bruised breasts. She wasn't sure how she had gotten home but she remembered her encounter with Akande and Master Clint.

"Go away," she told her sister. "Leave me alone."

"Are you sick?" Perla rattled the door. "What's wrong? Let me in."

"Go away," Marne said again. "I'm not going in today." Or ever again, she thought, imaging Lola's look when she discovered what had happened. There was no way she could keep her relationship with Akande a secret.

Then Marne remembered Master Clint's threat. She began shivering and couldn't stop herself.

She heard Perla return to the cooking room. Tears ran down Marne's face. She buried her head in the pillow, weeping as quietly as she could. Finally exhausted, she fell asleep.

She didn't hear her sister jimmying the lock open and didn't wake up again until she felt someone sitting on the edge of her bed, stroking her back. Turning to order Perla out of her room, she looked into Lola's face. No, she thought, dropping back on the pillow again. She couldn't bear it.

"Perla made you coffee." Lola pulled Marne's shoulder toward her. "Here, have a cup, then you can tell me what's going on."

"No," Marne cried, trying to pull away. Then she was caught by Lola's expression. She knew something. Maybe she already knew everything. "I can't." Marne shook her head. "I just can't."

"All right," Lola said. "Then sit up and listen." Marne sat up and leaned against her headboard accepting the cup of hot coffee. Perla lounged on the bed below Marne's feet.

"I don't know what happened yesterday, but this morning first Louis, then Akande, then Master Clint came looking for you. The Demon Spawn was quite insistent that you were working for him now. He told me to find you and send you to the *obanla's* offices."

Marne began to shake. After setting her half-empty coffee cup next to the pot on the side table, she wrapped her arms around herself. Maybe it had been a bad dream. Maybe Master Clint had not meant what he said to her.

Lola continued, "When I went into your office to find out what happened, you weren't there. The door was unlocked and your display was open, hanging in the air above your desk, so I thought you must be in the *obanla's* compound somewhere." She frowned, "However, no one had seen you. I was afraid something awful had happened, but before contacting the Hunter who guarded the compound, I called here. Perla told me something was wrong with you. She said you had locked yourself in your room and refused to get out of bed. That you weren't coming to work."

She looked at Marne. "Do you want to tell me what happened?"

Her sister handed her a piece of cloth. Marne blew her nose and wiped her eyes although tears continued to flow.

"Should I go back to the *obanla's* compound and interrogate my husband and his chief of staff?" Lola asked. "They said nothing was going on but I know them too well. I can get the story out of them if I have to." She took a sip of her coffee. "But I'd rather hear your side first."

Marne looked at her sister. She was only thirteen, barely into her waist beads. Not old enough to listen to what Marne would be telling Lola.

"Get out, Perla," Marne whispered.

Her sister protested.

"Go to the market or something," Marne said. "Don't come back until after midday. Iya Lola and I need to have a private conversation."

Marne listened as Perla slammed around the apartment, then out the front door.

Marne glanced at the woman who had taken her under her wing, teaching her first retail business and then the inner workings of the city council. The woman she had deceived. She realized that she had grown to love Lola as a second mother and wondered maybe she thought of Marne as a daughter. Now she had destroyed everything.

Wrapping her arms around herself again, Marne told Lola about her dalliance with Akande. She described the evening he taught her to drink wine. And the day the two of them stopped on the way to the meeting of the Hunters Guild.

"I-I didn't want it to happen," she stammered. "But I didn't know what to do."

Lola set her coffee cup on the table. "Can I sit next to you?"

When Marne nodded, the older woman scooted onto the bed. They sat side-by-side, leaning against the headboard.

"You know you're not the first girl my husband has seduced, don't you?" Lola put her arm around Marne and drew her close.

Although she only suspected the truth of what Lola told her, it wasn't a surprise.

"Do you have feelings for him?" Lola looked into Marne's tear-stained face.

Marne shook her head and then stopped to consider the question. She delighted in Dele's caresses, but Akande left her feeling defiled, as though his actions and her responses debased them both.

"No," she stammered. "He chose me and took liberties. I didn't know how to refuse him. I couldn't make myself not respond to him but afterward I wished it hadn't happened."

Lola was silent for a long time, playing with the edge of the coverlet she had drawn across her legs. This was the moment Marne feared. When her boss banished her from her business and from her life.

"You have been so good to me." Marne looked away. "I didn't mean to betray you and I'm so sorry." She wanted to throw herself into Lola's lap and beg her forgiveness.

"You're young and very beautiful." Lola squeezed Marne closer to herself. "You need to learn to deflect such attentions. There are men like my husband everywhere and we all have to defend ourselves against them."

It took a moment for Marne to realize what Lola said. She wasn't angry. Instead she was talking like an older sister—or a mother.

Marne refilled Lola's coffee. She turned toward this woman she loved and handed the cup to her, with both hands, the way one made a solemn offering. "*Modupue*, thank you." She used the spiritual language.

Lola took the cup as Marne offered it, in two hands in the sacred manner. "*Ashe O*," she responded, so be it. "And thank you for being honest. I know how difficult honesty is."

Lola sipped the coffee, staring across the room. "But there's more going on here than your relationship with my husband. Isn't there?"

Marne wanted to hide. She was surprised that her boss took such a tenderhearted view of what happened between herself and her husband. She expected a much different response. But maybe Lola knew more about last night's encounter with Akande and the Demon Spawn than she said. Perhaps they had threatened her, and she would punish Marne by allowing Master Clint to use her as his plaything. Marne shuddered again, thinking of how he smelled and how his chapped and calloused hands fondled her. She pulled her nightshirt away from her bruised nipples.

"Master Clint," Marne started, and then faltered. Taking a deep breath, she decided to tell the whole shameful story. "Master Clint discovered me in Akande's sitting room. We both had our shirts open and were playing with each other." She stopped to look at Lola who was staring into her cup. "That was all we did," Marne whispered. the older woman put her arm back around Marne's shoulder. Marne was reassured. Lola was like a mother to her. She hated having disappointed and deceived her. She had not wanted to have anything to do with Akande even though his wife might see it that way.

"That was how Master Clint found us. He came to where I was sitting and touched me, played with me, too. I was so scared. He looked like a beast." More tears flowed down Marne's face and onto Lola's blouse. She needed to keep talking. She had to get it out before she broke down again. "Master Clint said they should add me to our tribute. He said he wanted me to 'work' for him. He told me I couldn't hide. He would come looking for me."

Marne considered the man who had been attending the council meetings. She remembered the dragon crawling up Master Clint's arm. It looked frightening, evil. She wasn't the only assistant to the village council who cowered when he prowled the hallways. She guessed that the council members were afraid of him too, especially after he shot at Malik. Last night Akande and Louis watched as the Spawn leader fondled her, saying nothing to him.

"Don't make me go with him," Marne sobbed. "Please, I'll do anything, be anything you want, but please, don't give me to Master Clint."

"There, there," Lola hugged her, touching her hair, her back. "No one's going to give you away. I know this is hard, but you need to tell me everything." She pushed Marne, so they again sat side-by-side. "Where did he touch you?"

Marne waved her hands up and down her torso.

"Did he go below your waist beads, dear?" Lola's voice was kind.

"No, mostly my breasts, but also my belly. He kissed me, hard." Marne wondered whether her lips and mouth were swollen. They were sensitive.

"Did he injure you?"

"His hands were coarse, working man's hands, but he was gentle, except, except…"

"Except?" Lola probed.

"He bit me. Not a tender nip like Akande but sharp, cruel." She cradled her sore breast. "I think he intended it to hurt, and it still does. Oh, Lola," Marne sobbed. "Akande and Louis watched the whole thing. They didn't say a word. They let him do whatever he wanted. When he was finished and dismissed me, Louis told me not to tell you or anyone." Soon, she thought, everyone would know. What if her grandmother found out?

Marne stared down at her hands. "Are Akande and Master Clint friends? Would he let Master Clint take me for his own?"

"No, dear," Lola drew Marne back to her. "We won't let him take you."

"But, but how will you stop him? Louis could not keep him out of the sitting room, even though Akande told him not to disturb us. He didn't stop him and I don't think he could have. Master Clint wore that gun, even there. And he called Akande his friend."

"I don't know, dear," the councilwoman sighed. "I don't know why Master Clint called my husband his friend. None of us are friends with the Demon Spawn."

Marne remembered how the council members looked when they thought the Demon Spawn had shot Malik, the looks they gave each other passing in the hallway. The plans of the Hunters Guild had fallen apart when the gang had invaded Verdant Valley. They had to cancel their training. Besides, Lola had said there was no money for guns. What could they do?

Despite her promise, everyone was terrified. No one denied Master Clint or any member of the Demon Spawn anything. With that, Marne knew no one could protect her. Not Akande, one of the most powerful man in Verdant Valley, not the village council, not even Lola. If Master Clint wanted her, no one could stop him.

CHAPTER 9

Marne had not returned to the *obanla's* compound after the incident with Master Clint, but spent her days with her grandmother instead.

"I will borrow an assistant from Akande," Lola had told her. "He owes me that much, at least. You can come back when the rest of the Demon Spawn take their tribute and leave."

Marne was happy to be cleaning up the workshop and preparing for the delayed winter dyeing season. Most afternoons, her granny hosted groups for tea and conversation. Intermixed with those casual events that brought together women from around the town were meetings of the Sisterhood of the Moon. They were searching for a third way to defeat the Spawn and save Verdant Valley. They were trying to find the weak spot in the armor of the gang, the place where they could insert themselves to prevent violence and the loss that accompanied it.

Today Marne opened the door, greeting Jumoke, the first to arrive. Lola and Li'l Meg followed her. As before, the Spawn woman was dressed in black, looking like the night itself.

Marne and her granny prepared the hot tea and nibbles, setting cups and trays on the side tables. Meanwhile, Li'l Meg wandered around Granny's sitting room, touching the indigo cloth that covered the walls and chairs. She picked up, then put down Gladys's various scattered mementos. She looked interested in an old-fashioned photograph she found on a table pushed against the back wall. Marne knew it was a shrine to the memory of her mother, her granny's only daughter.

There was a shop off the square in Scarlet Dawn that produced photos on paper for the visitors that inundated the Reserve during the summer season. You could have your picture made in antique costumes, then the proprietor printed and framed it for you. It was an outmoded process, but the outsiders loved it. Before she got sick, Marne's mother had insisted that she and the girls have their photo taken with their granny. "Three generations of strong women," she had said as she presented the photograph to Granny afterwards. Marne kept a copy of the same picture beside her own bed. It had been on a similar small table in her mother's sitting room. But after she died, her father insisted that the girls clear the apartment of everything that reminded him of his former wife.

When Marne saw Li'l Meg handling the photograph she sucked in her breath. She didn't want the Demon Spawn touching anything of hers. But before she could say something, the woman returned the picture to its place.

When the women were settled with their drinks and nibbles, Jumoke patted the seat next to her on the sofa, inviting Marne to join them.

"I know that you are busy," she said to Marne. "These two," she nodded toward Lola and Marne's granny, "have conspired to keep you away from the work you should be doing out at the shrine."

Marne hung her head. She hadn't been out to the forest since her vision at the Market Board meeting. Jumoke knew how she had filled her days. It was not her commitments that had kept her from going out to the shrine, but fear. She had not told her godmother, but she could not bear the thought of seeing more blood and destruction.

However, it didn't appear that the shrine was Jumoke's concern. "Tell us what you have been doing," she said, cutting her eyes toward Li'l Meg who sat glaring at them, specifically Marne. Then Marne realized this was another performance for the Spawn woman.

"Well," she began, not sure what Jumoke wanted her to say, "things have been busy at the *obanla's* compound, especially now that Josephine got married and moved away. I'm Lola's only assistant now." The Spawn woman appeared to be focused on cleaning her nails with her dagger. Marne glanced at her granny, "And I've been helping Granny with her tea parties, since she hasn't yet fired up the workshop."

"And what do you do the rest of your time, sweetie?" Jumoke asked.

"I help cook and clean for my father?" The question in Marne's voice betrayed her confusion. Jumoke knew about her home life, maybe better than anyone other than Granny. What was she asking her?

"Oh," Jumoke said, "your mother is teaching you to keep house?"

Marne stared across the room. Jumoke knew her mother died over four years ago. She knew she and her sister had been maintaining her father's apartment since then. Why the nonsense questions?

"My mother's dead," Marne answered, her voice flat, emotionless. She refused to betray the continuing pain of her mother's absence. Not here. Not in front of the flinty Spawn woman. "She been dead more than four years." Marne looked at Li'l Meg, who was staring at her. "I was almost twelve when we buried her. My sister, Perla, and I have been maintaining my father's household since then. Perla's fourteen now and still in school."

"I thought your father remarried," Lola said, again asking a question Marne was sure she knew the answer to.

Marne nodded. "He did, but his new wife is too delicate to do housework. She's happy to let us continue our cooking and cleaning." Marne tried to keep the annoyance out of her voice. Then she wondered whether any of the women noticed that she never named the woman who lived with her father. She was only a little older than Marne herself and, as far as she was concerned, didn't deserve to be recognized as any name other than her relationship role.

"I see." Lola held out her cup in a silent request for more tea.

Glad to be released from whatever game Jumoke was playing, Marne retreated to the cooking room. When she returned, her heart skipped a beat when she realized Li'l Meg was again holding the photograph.

After Marne had refilled everyone's cups and set the teapot on the table next to her granny, the Spawn woman held up the photo. "Was this your mother?" she asked.

Marne nodded. "That's Granny and my mother. The two little girls are Perla and me. That was right before Mommy got sick."

The woman looked back at the photograph. There was a longing in her eyes that softened and humanized her features. After a long moment, she returned the photo to its place on the table.

"We've all lost someone," Jumoke said, as though she was changing the subject. "Marne's mother was Gladys's only child. Lola's sons remain in their father's compound, but her daughter died giving birth to her only grandchild. The boy and its father live far away. Both she and I have watched our parents sicken and die." She glanced around, sharing each woman's grief.

Marne stared into her lap, the pain of her mother's loss as fresh as the day they buried her. Tears leaked out of her eyes.

Jumoke held a hanky out to Li'l Meg. "What about you, sweetie?" she said. "Who have you lost?"

The room was silent. Marne didn't want to stare into the woman's grief, but she could not look away from her weeping.

After a moment, Li'l Meg took a bright red bandanna out of her pocket, blew her nose, and dried her eyes. Then she jerked to her feet, grabbed Lola's hand, and pulled her up.

"Don't you ever do that to me again," Li'l Meg hissed before pushing Lola out of the door ahead of her. Everyone jumped when it slammed behind the two of them.

Marne's granny stood and refilled everyone's cup. "That went well," she said. She looked at Marne and smiled. "Thank you, dear. I know that wasn't easy and I couldn't warn you, but you were just right."

She raised her teacup in a salute. "To the third way."

"To the third way," the other women responded, raising their cups.

The following day Marne and her grandmother were tidying up Granny's small home. They worked in a companionable silence preparing for another of her tea parties. The peace was interrupted by the sound of motorcycles turning off the main road and making their way toward them.

Marne peeked out the window above the door to see who was pulling to a stop in the front garden. "It's Master Clint," she stuttered, fear paralyzing her. Had he found her at last?

"Go to the back," her granny commanded. "Hide in the shrine room. I'll take care of this."

She raced down the hall but stopped before her granny's shrine. What were the Demon Spawn doing here? She had to know. Turning around she crept toward the sitting room. Near the doorway, she slid down the wall to squat on her haunches, just out of sight.

She heard her granny open the door.

"Where is she?" Master Clint demanded.

Marne trembled. She should escape to the workshop but she could not move.

"Please come in and sit down," Granny said. Marne imagined her motioning them into the sitting room. "Would you like something to drink? Coffee? Tea?"

The two Demon Spawn stomped in.

"Where's that girl of yours?" Master Clint growled. "I know she's out here. Go get her."

"You mean my granddaughter? I think she works at the *obanla's*."

"We know she's here," Li'l Meg repeated. "I've seen her. Now do yourself a favor and call her." She paused, "You have such nice things. You don't want us to have to go looking for her."

Marne started when the sound of some small thing crashed against the wall near her head. Granny gasped, but said nothing.

"I don't think I can help you," Granny's voice wavered. "Have you talked to Lola, the councilwoman?"

"Don't mess with me," Clint snarled. "I don't have all day here."

Another of memento shattered.

Marne pulled herself into a tight ball. Tears streamed down her face and she covered her mouth with her hands to keep her whimpering from escaping. Why hadn't she done as she was told and escaped? What would the Demon Spawn do to her when he found her?

Expecting more keepsakes to hit the wall, she was surprised to hear the sharp sound of a slap and her grandmother's cry.

"Clint is not a patient person," Li'l Meg said. "You don't want to make him angry."

Another slap and another cry from her granny.

"Where is she?" Master Clint shouted.

After a moment, she heard a loud crack, then Granny screaming in agony. Without thinking, Marne stood up and showed herself in the doorway.

"I'm here," she whispered. "Leave her alone."

Clint turned to her, his face still red with rage. "Why were you hiding from me, darlin'?" He waved at her grandmother, who sat cradling one arm in the other. "Look what you made me do. Your poor gran has broken her arm."

Marne stepped toward her granny, but Li'l Meg caught her and pushed her to Master Clint. He held her by the shoulders.

"Have you been crying, darlin'?" He asked, his voice softening. He traced the line of her tears on her cheeks and then pulled her jaw up so she had to look at him. His eyes were hard, an evil chartreuse color. When she glanced away, he slapped her. "Don't you ever hide from me again." Now he sounded harsh, cold. "I don't like defiant women. Do you understand, darlin'?"

When she nodded, he shoved her toward Li'l Meg. "Get her stuff. We need to get going."

The woman picked up a small black bag and pushed Marne down the hallway. "You're going on an excursion," she said. "Let's get what you need."

In the narrow back room, she turned to Marne. "I don't know why Clint's taken a shine to you, but he has. Don't be stupid. He can hurt you really, really bad." She threw the bag at her. "You can take whatever fits in this."

Marne stuffed the few things she was keeping out here into the bag.

"And quit your bawling," the Spawn Meg sneered. "It makes your ugly face even uglier."

When the bag was full, the woman led Marne back through the house, past her granny, and out to the motorcycles where Master Clint was waiting.

"Have you ever ridden one of these before?" she asked.

Marne shook her head. Li'l Meg handed her a helmet and helped put it on. Then she pushed her onto the rear seat of Master Clint's cycle and wrapped her arms around his waist. He reached behind him and pulled her closer. Then he forced her hands lower and she felt the bulge between his legs.

"Hold on tight, darlin'," his voice came through a speaker in her helmet. She tightened her arms as they roared back up the drive and out onto the main road.

It was almost dark by the time Meg, Clint, and Marne rode into the Demon Spawn encampment. It was several miles north of the secondary highway used to leave Verdant Valley. Sheltered behind a bluff were the vague shapes of trailers and motor homes parked in a haphazard fashion.

Clint pulled up close to one of the larger structures near what looked like the central plaza. People were sitting around a campfire on unsteady chairs and blankets. They talked in the boisterous manner of those who thought they could still drink more.

While Li'l Meg unloaded their bags and other equipment, Clint led Marne to the fire. Most of those lounging around were men. Young men, middle-aged men. Even a few white-haired men.

"Hey, Clint," someone shouted, "did you bring us some dark meat from your little excursion?" A general hooting and whistling followed.

Master Clint pushed her into the circle of light. "This here's mine," he said, rubbing his coarse palms along her bare arms, resting them on her hips. "If I find out one of you cowboys so much as laid a finger on her, I'll chop it off. No fingers, no hands, no tongue, and certainly no dick."

Several of the drinkers made rude gestures simulating intercourse and laughed. Clint growled.

"Yes, sir," someone called. "She's yours, and yours alone."

"Yup," voices around the fire responded. "She's yours, and yours alone."

"Pity," said a deep voice and the others laughed.

Then he spun her away from them and marched her to the trailer. She saw a figure that appeared to be Meg moving around inside. She wondered about the relationship between Clint and the woman, who did not appear to be much older than Marne herself. They didn't act like husband and wife although she wasn't sure any longer how spouses where supposed to act.

As they approached the trailer, the door flew open. "What happened to our share of the last tribute?" Meg shouted. "We've been cleaned out."

"I gave it to Tommy and Joyce when we left," Clint barked. "I didn't expect to be back before the next shipment."

"Well, I can't cook air in here. Go see if she has anything we can eat. I'm starving."

He pushed Marne toward the trailer and then turned to retrace his steps through the encampment.

"Get in here," Meg called.

Marne looked around. Her eyes had adjusted to the darkness but all she saw were vague shapes and several campfires.

"Don't you go thinkin' of running away," the woman said. "We're fifty miles from anywhere and you won't survive out there in the dark. You run and he might just be pissed enough to let you go. That'd be a long, slow death." She turned and went back inside.

For much of the seemingly endless ride from her granny's, she had thought about her decision to give herself up to Master Clint. She saw where this would end. She wasn't ignorant of the ways of men and women and the Demon Spawn hadn't been shy about his intentions for her. Taking a deep breath and squaring her shoulders, she followed Li'l Meg into the trailer.

Li'l Meg had not allowed her to touch or even speak to her granny when she had led Marne away from the tiny house. But Granny said goodbye with her eyes. She had also raised her good hand in a three-fingered salute. They had ridden far from Verdant Valley before Marne realized what Granny had tried to tell her. "Remember. Search for a third way."

She had paid little attention to the conversation between Clint and Meg as they rode through the desert highlands of the Republic. She didn't know where the homeland of the Demon Spawn was, but she was sure that was where they were going. Master Clint was taking her into the heart of the mysterious gang that had been persecuting her people for years. As a member of the Sisterhood of the Moon, she would neither capitulate nor fight. She would find a third way out of this situation.

Inside the trailer, she was surprised to see the evidence of a woman's touch. She knew how a space looked when men lived alone and it was not true of this residence. Was Li'l Meg his wife? Lover? What did she think about him bringing her into their home?

Meg had stripped out of her leather jacket and pants and stood now in a simple tee-shirt and men's boxer shorts.

"Sit." She gestured toward the sofa in what appeared to be the main room. She sat in a side chair. "He won't be gone long, and we need to talk."

Marne perched on the edge of the lumpy cushion. This was it, she thought, this was when she found out what was in store for her.

"My father is not an evil man," Meg said.

Her father? Li'l Meg was Master Clint's daughter. Where was her mother?

Marne looked at her.

"He will expect absolute obedience from you. Inside," Meg waved her hand toward the rear of the trailer where Marne assumed the sleeping rooms must be, "but especially out there." Her gesture included the surrounding encampment. "They don't call him the Enforcer for nothing."

"Look at me," she said to Marne, who was staring into her lap ashamed of where she knew this was going.

Marne straightened her back and raised her eyes.

"Do you understand what I'm saying?"

Marne nodded.

"I don't know why he's brought you here," Meg shook her head. "He needs a woman, not a scared little girl. He likes strong women if you can find that within yourself. But, if you cross him, he'll punish you. Take it from me," she sighed, "he can be merciless."

Marne nodded again. She needed to survive.

"I put your bag in the back bedroom." Meg pointed to the rear of the trailer with her eyes. "Go wash your face and clean yourself."

Before she could move, door slammed open. Master Clint had returned.

Marne's first evening with the Demon Spawn had not been as dreadful as she had expected. Clint brought with him another couple whom he introduced as Tommy and Joyce. The man was tall and sinewy with skin the color of freshly mowed hay. A bright wine-colored birthmark spilled across the left side of his face. The woman, who appeared to be his wife from the way she talked and moved, was almost as tall and thin but with dark hair and a pale complexion.

They brought dishes full of steaming food and set them on the table in the kitchen and dining area. The two newcomers watched as Clint, Meg, and Marne ate. The meal was strange, tasteless, not unpleasant. Marne listened as the conversation swirled around her. Demon Spawn caught up on gossip of the encampment. No one spoke to her or explained her presence.

After Joyce had helped Meg clean up, the five of them moved to the sitting area. Clint sat next to Marne on the sofa with his arm draped over her shoulder and left knee pressed against her right. She smelled the dust from their ride with just a hint of the desert and below that a masculine odor. At one point the Spawn seemed to be talking about Verdant Valley but their conversation appeared coded, leaving Marne ignorant.

After a while, Joyce gathered up her dishes and led her husband away. Meg gave Marne a hard stare as if to remind her of what she had said earlier. Then she made her way to the back of the trailer, switching off lights as she went.

Clint waved his hand and the lamps lowered to a soft glow. He turned toward Marne. He had not said a word to her since before they arrived at the encampment. She realized that she hadn't cleaned up from her ride through the desert or washed her tear-stained face.

She stared at her hands, folded together in her lap. Now she would find out what Master Clint was really like. She sent a silent prayer to Oshun, the most erotic of the Orisha, to guide her in what she intended to do.

He reached out and pulled her chin up, forcing her to look into his eyes. He leaned forward to kiss her and then drew her closer while he explored her mouth. Determined to go ahead with her plan, she responded in kind, pressing her tongue against his.

"Darlin'," he moaned, then pushed her away. He grabbed the hem of her tee-shirt and yanked it up and over her head. He raised it to his face, inhaling her odor before flinging it across the room.

He cupped her breasts, licking his lips. Before he could lean forward, she brought her hands up between his, pushing them apart. She reached forward to unbutton his shirt, pulling the hem up and out of his pants. She swept the shirt and vest aside, and placed her palms on his chest, massaging him. Without dropping her eyes from his, she put her forefinger in her mouth, and then drew circles around his nipple. When he responded, she pinched and held it while reaching up to touch a finger from her other hand to his lips. He suckled like a hungry infant. But once her finger was wet, she withdrew it to circle his other nipple. He closed his eyes and released another moan.

He grabbed her breasts again, pinching the nipples until they responded. When he leaned forward, she caught his head in her hands, bringing his mouth to hers. He sucked and nipped on her bottom lip. Then he dropped his mouth to the breast he had bitten when he had found her in Akande's sitting room. It had mostly healed but was still tender. Her moan as he pulled it between his lips was not entirely fabricated as pain and pleasure battled for supremacy.

She slid her fingertips down his chest, circling his belly on their way toward his belt. Pinching and rubbing her sore breast, he moved to the other side. He was a greedy infant, nursing with single-minded intensity.

When she could not stand it any longer, she nudged his head. He resisted, scraping his teeth against the most sensitive part of her nipple. She cried out, and then encircled his nipple with her own mouth, nipping him as aggressively as he had her. He attempted to push her away, but she defied his half-hearted efforts.

He stretched forward to unbutton her jeans, but she swatted his hand, distracting him by attacking him again. She massaged him through the fabric of his trousers but made no movement toward releasing him. He moaned and threw himself back on the sofa. He lay still as she assessed him. His eyes were closed, and he was panting. His face had taken on a reddish hue and his thin pink lips had become thicker, darker. By tomorrow his nipples would be as sore as hers had been less than a week ago.

She leaned forward flicking her tongue over first one nipple and then the other. Before he finished his sigh, she caught the right one between her teeth while pinching the left between her fingernails.

His eye flew open, and he tried to sit up. But she pushed him down with while cupping the bulge straining the fabric of his jeans. He fell back and stared at her. When she was sure she had his full attention, she stood.

Licking her fingers she touched her breasts. He watched as she slid her hands across her belly. With aching slowness she undid the button of her pants and released the zipper. She saw his fingers twitching, but she shook her head. She would not allow him to touch her now.

When he reached toward his own belt buckle, she glared at him and slapped his hand. He pulled it away, content to follow her lead. Now she was at a crossroads. For the moment she was in charge. But she knew how quickly that control could be lost. She considered what she wanted and how she could achieve her objective.

Marne liked dominating and she liked being the tease. She had learned that about herself while playing with Dele and those other boys during summer. Now was the ultimate test of where her teasing led.

CHAPTER 10

Marne was slow to waken, waves of delight mixed with anguish rolling through her. She opened her eyes to discover she wasn't at home in her own sleeping room, but somewhere else. She turned toward the light peeking through the edges of the window covering. The pain of her breast brushing against the bed covering brought her fully awake and reminded her where she was. She smiled. The third way was much more pleasant than she had expected.   After dominating Master Clint in the sitting room, she was prepared for him to savage her in the sleeping room. However, he had been a thoughtful and attentive lover. He called her "darlin'" and other pet names. At one point, he used a warm cloth to wash off the dust of their ride, the tracks left by her earlier tears, and the juices of their copulation. She had discovered, the more she treated him with a mixture of domination and disdain, the more solicitous he was — eager to please her or to bend to her demands.

As she was falling asleep, nestled into the circle of his body, she had wondered what the morning would bring. Would he return to the stony persona he exhibited in the *obanla*'s compound or would he change? Would he have a different attitude toward her and her people?

Now, rolling out of bed and making her way to the bathing room, she wondered if Master Clint was also feeling the effects of their night together. She was sure the tips of his breasts were as tender as hers.

Humming a song of thanksgiving to Oshun, the Orisha of sexuality she had called upon to sustain her during the night, she washed herself. Digging through the bag Li'l Meg had made her pack she found some clean-enough clothes.

Finally, she couldn't put it off any longer. She stood in front of the door separating her from whatever this day held and adjusted her beads, so they rode unencumbered above the waistband of her pants. Throughout the coming day, every time she moved Master Clint would hear the beads clicking together, gossiping about his night with her. Taking a deep breath, she squared her shoulders. I am a Sister of the Moon, she thought, and the daughter of both Yemaya and Oshun.

"Well, well, well," Li'l Meg greeted her as she made her way toward the kitchen from the sleeping room. Waving her toward a chair around the table in the cooking space, Li'l Meg handed Marne a cup. The warm liquid was the weakest coffee Marne had ever tasted. But it was hot, and she swallowed it.

Li'l Meg stared at her. "Are you a witch?" she asked. "Because I believe you have bewitched my father. I've never seen him like this."

Marne returned her look but didn't respond. She remembered what her granny had told her about women's witchcraft substance. She felt she had performed a kind of witchcraft on both Master Clint and herself, but she wasn't ready to explain that to Li'l Meg.

"People have told me how he used to be, before..." Meg's voice dropped. "What did you do to him?"

Marne took another sip of the so-called coffee and said, "We only did what men and women do. I gave him what he wanted. I hope now you will take me home and quit harassing my people." She was surprised to hear her whole plan tumble out of her mouth.

"Take you home?" Li'l Meg laughed. "By the look on his face this morning, he's never letting you leave. Unless you've got a transport spell in there somewhere, this is your new home."

Marne looked around, appraising the trailer. "Where is your mother?" she asked, looking back at her companion.

A dark cloud passed over Li'l Meg's face. She looked into her own cup. "My mother's not here anymore," she mumbled. "She died. Over a year ago."

Marne scooted her chair around and draped her arm around Li'l Meg's shoulder. Last night she had felt the power of Oshun but today she needed to be the comforting touch of Yemaya, the Mother of All. "What happened?" she asked, her voice a mere whisper as though Li'l Meg was about to reveal a great secret.

"You don't know," Li'l Meg said. "Your people have plenty to eat but we don't. Ever since Junior disappeared, we're always hungry, even the children. Mommy always saw that Clint and I were fed even if it meant she went hungry. Then she fell pregnant. Her half-starved body couldn't support the baby. When it died inside her, no one helped her and she died, too." Tears streamed down the girl's face.

Marne pulled Li'l Meg closer until Meg's head rested like a baby's on her breasts. She gasped at the stab of pain, but still reached up to caress the girl's hair. Remembering her anguish when her own mother had died, she wondered when Master Clint would take a new wife as her father had.

Marne continued petting Li'l Meg and murmuring comforting words while the girl wept. Her tears soaked through Marne's thin tee-shirt and dampened her skin.

When Li'l Meg ran out of tears, she sat up, wiping her runny nose with the hem of her shirt. Her face was red and blotchy.

"I lost my mother, too," Marne said. "It was almost five years ago, but I still miss her every day."

Before she could say more, they heard a step on the stairs outside.

"He's back." Li'l Meg jumped to her feet and ran toward the sleeping rooms.

Marne stood to follow her. She needed to change her shirt but as she passed the outside door it was flung open.

"Whoa there, darlin'," Master Clint said, catching her in his arms. "Don't you go running away, now."

She took a deep breath before looking up at him. Who did she need to be now?

Marne pulled away from Master Clint, who planted a juicy kiss on her cheek before she was out of his reach.

"She's a feisty one," he laughed to another man who followed him up the stairs and into the trailer. Turning back toward her, he pressed his palm against the front of her tear-soaked tee-shirt. He frowned and said, "Go change, then scoot on back here. Duke has a few questions for you."

She met Li'l Meg in the hallway. The girl's eyes were still swollen but her face was no longer flushed. Marne ran her palm along Li'l Meg's arm and squeezed her hand as they passed.

"Meg," Clint shout, "Where are you, girl? Get your lazy self out here."

Marne found her shirt and pants from yesterday tossed into a pile on the floor in the back bedroom. Since that shirt was cleaner than anything in her bag, she shook out as many of the wrinkles as she could before putting it on.

When she walked from the back of the trailer, Master Clint and the man Marne recognized as Master Duke were lounging in the sitting room, sipping beers. Meg refilled Marne's coffee cup as she passed by the cooking area. Marne would have liked the comfort of a beer but accepted the hot cup with a nod of thanks.

"Come here, darlin'." Master Clint patted a narrow space on the sofa. He had to pull his legs together to allow her to slide between him and the armrest. As soon as she sat, he spread his legs back apart, pinning her beside him. He dropped his palm to her thigh in an obvious sign of his possession of her as his odor of dust and desert and manhood surrounded her.

She pushed herself as far into the corner of the sofa as possible, cradling her coffee in her lap. Ignoring Master Clint, she pretended not to notice his legs, the bulge in his pants, or his touch. She didn't want him touching her, but she didn't remove his hand, not wanting to embarrass him in front of the man she assumed was his superior.

Meg, carrying her own beer, sat on a chair opposite Marne and her father.

"Clint thinks a group of your people believe they can fight us instead of giving us our tribute." Master Duke looked at her and frowned. She remembered the day he had invaded the council meeting and Master Clint had shot at Akande. A shiver ran down her spine. She shook her head as she considered her options. That day she had thought Master Clint was the most evil of men. But he was subservient to this man. Master Duke neither lusted after her nor needed a mother's touch. He would be more difficult to deal with than either Master Clint or Li'l Meg.

"What do you know about that?" he demanded.

Master Clint patted her leg as if to reassure her, but she knew he couldn't protect her against Master Duke. A chant for Eleggua, the trickster Orisha, came to her. Her people said Eleggua opened and closed the doors of possibility. She remembered the prayer that ended, "May the owner of gossip not lead me astray."

Before she responded, Master Clint said, "Akande told me some people were trying to raise an army against us. Is that true, darlin'?"

She turned frightened eyes toward him. Had Akande betrayed them or were these men fishing for information? Swallowing hard, she nodded. She hoped Eleggua would help her use the truth to lead these people astray.

"The Hunters Guild was trying to gather people to fight," she said.

Master Duke snorted as though the idea was ludicrous.

"But they couldn't continue after you and your..." she paused, "... ah, friends arrived."

"Did they think they could overpower us?" Master Duke laughed. If he imagined farmers with pitchforks and machetes against the guns of his gang, he wasn't far from reality.

"I don't think so," she said, "but they had to do something."

Master Duke shook his head as if amazed at the audacity of her people.

For a moment, Marne watched the three Spawn sit drinking their beer.

"What about your grandmother's third way?" Li'l Meg asked.

Marne drank the insipid coffee and sent another silent prayer to Eleggua.

"There are some women." She drew out her response as if reluctant to speak. "They call themselves the Sisterhood of the Moon. They are always looking for what they call the third way to handle the issues that arise among my people."

"Do these women have weapons? Are they Amazons like the warrior women in the stories?" Master Duke asked.

Marne shook her head. "Oh, no." She glanced toward Li'l Meg. "You've met them. They are mostly market women and artisans."

Li'l Meg nodded, but said nothing. Marne wondered what she was thinking. The Sisterhood had been less than kind to her.

"Are you saying these women think they can use this third way against us?" Master Clint growled.

Marne nodded, giving him her sweetest smile, wiggling as though nervous. She was sure Master Clint heard the soft jingle of her waist beads. He looked from her face to where the beads sat, hidden under her tee shirt. She resisted the urge to glance at his manhood, straining against his pants. He didn't yet realize what she had done to him.

Master Duke harrumphed, then laughed. After a moment Li'l Meg and Master Clint joined him.

"Malik the Milquetoast is raising an army of market women and artisans," Master Duke laughed, "against us, against the Demon Spawn?"

Marne smiled and nodded again as the three of them continued laughing.

When they had worn themselves out, Master Duke ogled her. Now his smile made him look like a cat that had cornered its prey and was looking for a lively tussle before killing it. He winked at her. Marne knew she might have won this scrimmage but there were more clashes to come.

"That tells me everything I need to know," Master Duke said, standing. "Clint, show your new plaything around before sending her back where she belongs. And you will send her back." He gave Master Clint a hard look. "Be sure she sees our battle corps before she goes. She needs to know what her people are up against."

At the door, he turned back toward Marne. "Market women and artisans," he laughed at her. "Like taking candy from a baby."

After Master Duke left, Master Clint pulled Marne to himself, kissing her. "Oh, darlin'," he said, when she shoved him away. "Didn't you miss me?"

She glanced at Meg who was picking up the now empty beer containers. He followed her eyes.

"Make yourself scarce, Meg," he hissed. "This one and I have some, ah, business to take care of." He found Marne's hand and placed it on his bulging crotch.

She traced the outline of his erection through his pants, then lifted her hand to his chest. He moaned as his nipple responded to her touch. Yes, he was as sore from last night's play as she was. Taking his head between her hands she touched his lips to hers. Then pulled back.

"Master Duke said you should show me around. I'd like to see this place." She smiled sweetly as though unaware of the desire raging through him.

"That can wait," he groaned, pulling her toward him.

She nudged him onto the sofa and crawled into his lap, resting her buttocks on his thighs. Reaching forward, she massaged his chest through this shirt while grinding herself against him. "Hmm," she said, "you like that, don't you?"

He closed his eyes and moaned again. Tweaking his other nipple, she swung herself off him. She was almost through the outside door before he caught up with her. He grabbed her arm and swung her around to face him.

"Where do you think you're going?" he growled, flushed and angry-looking.

"For a walk. I want to see where you brought me."

He pulled her back into the trailer and slammed the door. "Not now."

She saw again the man who was willing to shoot Akande. Had she pushed him too far?

She turned to face him. "You're scaring me. I'm too sore to play with you and I'm afraid of what you and Master Duke are planning. I want to take a walk."

"Mmm, darlin'," he murmured, "don't tease me and you won't need to be scared. Now come back here and finish what you've started." He pushed her toward the sitting room.

She pulled back. "No, I won't."

He raised his hand as though to slap her. She caught it.

"Hit me," she whispered, "and you'll never again see the girl from last night."

Rage raced across his face. She had only her will against his strength. Nothing she could do would stop him from taking whatever he wanted. He was Master Clint the Enforcer. She was just a frightened young girl who had, perhaps, gotten herself in too deep. What made her think she could control this uncontrollable man? Last night she was Oshun, the patron of love and pleasure, but today she was following the path of Eleggua, the trickster.

Still holding his hand, she dampened her other index finger, then ran it over his lips. When he tried to suck it into his own mouth, she pulled it away and held it back against his lips to silence any protest. She watched the anger drain first from his eyes, then from around his mouth. His face changed from an angry flush back to its normal pale *oyinbo* color. The Enforcer receded back beneath the persona of the hungry boy.

"Darlin'," he moaned, "what have you done to me?"

She smiled and leaned forward to kiss him, pulling his lower lip into her mouth. "Waiting won't hurt you." She put as much promise into her voice as she was able.

He shook his head. His rage had drained away at her touch.

"Now, let's go outside. Meg," she called out, "Master Clint is going to show me around. Please come along."

Only silence came from Li'l Meg's sleeping room. After a moment her head poked out. "You're what?" She looked from one to the other, Master Clint's hand still caught in Marne's. He still looked dazed, confused. "Just a minute," Li'l Meg said.

Soon they were standing outside the trailer, Marne holding the father's hand on one side and the daughter's on the other.

Marne's tour highlighted what Li'l Meg had told her earlier. The encampment was full of powerful men and emaciated women and children. It appeared that most of them had never seen someone from the Reserve with their dark skin and curly hair. Everyone stared at her, but Master Clint's possessive scowl kept most of them away.

At first she was content to walk between the two *oyinbo*. But then she began greeting the children. Releasing Master Clint and Li'l Meg hands, she squatted before one child. He held out his hand as if to touch her.

"Bobbie, no," his mother said, looking not at Marne but at Master Clint standing behind her.

Marne held out her arm to the child. "Here," she said. "I feel the same as you."

He touched her with his index finger and smiled when she returned the gesture, touching her forefinger to his cheek. His eyes widened when she leaned forward and planted a kiss on his forehead. He giggled and ran to his mother, who smiled at Marne as she stood.

Before long children surrounded her, touching her arms and patting her springy coils. She returned their touches by catching them in deep hugs and covering their dirty faces with sloppy kisses. The children and their mothers had the waif-like look of people who didn't have enough to eat. Marne wondered what had happened to the tribute Verdant Valley had already sent to the Demon Spawn.

A jumble of trailers was clustered around the remains of campfires like the one Master Clint had led her to when they had first arrived. Had that been last night? So much had happened to her.

After a while, Master Clint led them toward his own trailer. But instead of going back inside, he handed Marne her helmet and lifted her onto the back of his motorcycle.

"We're going out to the pits," he told Li'l Meg. "I'll be hungry when we get back. The mechanic's been looking' for you. Pop on over and see what he's got we can eat. He owes you that much."

Moments later, Marne and Clint were rolling through the camp, twisting this way and that to avoid the clusters of people following their progress. It was obvious from the way people had watched them while they were walking and now as they rode among them that Master Clint was an important man. These people feared him and perhaps Li'l Meg as well. For a moment she shrank into herself, the wolf of her own fear gnawing at her belly. She had to stay strong if she was going to survive here.

Riding beyond the encampment, Master Clint followed a narrow track around a small rise and into a natural amphitheater. Groups of young men and woman were watching different performances. Unlike the people in the encampment, these people barely acknowledged Master Clint or his companion.

He led her to the closest cluster and pushed his way to the front of the group. The smell of human sweat was overwhelming. Marne reached up to protect her mouth and nose from the stench, then dropped her hand. If Master Clint had brought her here to frighten her, which she thought he had, she had to control her responses.

In an open space in the middle the crowd, two men were engaging in a wrestling match.

Like most young women, Marne had enjoyed watching the men of her village prove themselves in the form of wrestling they called "the game." This was a different style of fighting, without the finesse that made the game so intriguing. However, these two men were beautifully formed without the gaunt look of the women and children she had seen earlier.

As she watched, she realized that members of the crowd were betting on the contestants. It soon became clear that the crowd favored the stronger man although Marne saw that the technique of the smaller, younger man was better. She would have bet on him instead.

Before the conclusion of the match, Master Clint drew her away. Without comment, he walked her past group after group of people engaging in different styles of hand-to-hand combat. There was more wrestling, but also a form of barehanded boxing, and fights with several sizes of knives.

He took her to another spot. At first it looked chaotic, people forming into groups and individuals wandering between several structures. They were stalking each other. Some had guns. The others carried sticks.

When Master Clint led Marne to higher ground, she saw the buildings were similar to those back home in Verdant Valley. Then she realized she was observing a mock battle between her people and the Demon Spawn. Soon the Spawn forces overwhelmed their opponents. The bodies of those representing her people were soon scattered on the ground, defeated by the superior forces of the gang.

The hot sun beat on Marne's unprotected head and she felt faint. All she'd had to eat since last night's dinner was Li'l Meg's weak coffee.

A bell began to toll. The combatants representing the Spawn raced toward an open space on one edge of the space. The gun-carrying Demon Spawn shot at a set of targets on the far side of the field. Then the "dead" villagers rose up and raced across the field to attack the same targets with their sticks. In a matter of minutes they reduced images of the village council members to scrap.

This is what Master Duke wanted her to see, his forces annihilating her people. Her head began to swim. The chant from her vision at the Market Guild meeting rang in her ears, "Blood. Blood. Blood." In a moment, she was overwhelmed. She collapsed into darkness.

CHAPTER 11

Marne stifled a scream when her eyes fluttered open. Master Clint's face hung above her, covered in blood. Before the vision faded she saw that his throat had been slit from ear-to-ear. Had her own hand dealt that fatal blow?

As his face returned to its naturally pale color, he cradled one side of her face.

"Welcome back, darlin'," he smiled. "You gave us quite a scare."

She was in Master Clint's trailer, lying on the sofa. She remembered watching the simulated skirmish and the death, not just of her own people but of everyone on the battlefield.

As she sat up, Li'l Meg pressed a cup of the insipid *oyinbo* coffee into her hands. Marne would have preferred the cool herbal water her granny had given her when she'd had a similar vision at the Market Board meeting. Sipping the steaming hot liquid, she was grateful for this small act of kindness. She had almost forgotten the deadly nature of her interactions with the Demon Spawn. She must not forget Master Clint was not just a man she was playing the game of seduction with. He was also one of the most important men in this group that was preparing to destroy her village.

"Are you feeling better?" he asked, concern tingeing his voice.

She nodded. What would he do now? Would he force her to watch the real battle between her people and his? A fight that neither side would win, regardless of what those young men out there believed? In spite of what she had told Master Duke earlier, the Hunters Guild was continuing to prepare to repulse the Demon Spawn, even if it meant their annihilation. The Sisterhood of the Moon were the only ones standing between both groups and utter destruction.

"Do you remember what you saw?" Master Clint frowned. "Before you collapsed?"

Marne nodded.

"We will take our tribute," he said. "No one can stop us. Do you understand, darlin'?"

She nodded again. Better than he knew.

"What happened to what you've taken already?" she asked. Li'l Meg had said the people were starving, and she'd seen it in the gaunt faces of the encampment. But Verdant Valley had been sending trucks to the Demon Spawn for several years. Where had all that food gone?

"Duke took it," Li'l Meg called from the cooking area. "I'm sure you saw he and his soldiers are well-fed." Marne had noticed the difference between the women and children in the encampment and the young people out at the battleground.

"You know Duke's taken care of us," Master Clint yelled, obviously hearing the anger in Li'l Meg's voice.

"After it was too late." She slammed a cabinet door shut.

Master Clint's face reddened. When he moved to stand up, Marne leaned forward and put her hand on his knee. She remembered what Li'l Meg had said about her mother. The girl was still grieving. And, Marne guessed, so was Master Clint.

"Duke's fixin' to sell most of the tribute to the City," the Spawn woman said, "to buy new cycles and guns for his friends. He says everyone will get a share of the next load." She let her voice fade away.

Marne threw herself back onto the sofa in an attitude of despair. "What can we do?" she sobbed. "You are plotting to kill us, all of our men, all of our women, all of our children."

"No, no, darlin'." Master Clint pulled her onto his lap and kissed her forehead in a gesture reminiscent of the kisses she had given the little ones earlier. "Your people are goin' to do as we ask, then everything'll be fine. We'll get what we need and their lives will go on." He leaned forward to kiss her lips, but she pushed him away.

She looked across the sitting room to where Li'l Meg sat watching them.

"Every year your tribute causes hunger in the reserve. Now you will kill us. Not just my Verdant Valley but everyone."

"That's not true," Li'l Meg said. "We've been to your village. No one is starving." She paused for a long time, her eyes shining with unshed tears. "We are dying. You've seen our children. How many of those little ones do you think will survive the coming cold?"

Marne slid off Master Clint's lap and tried to push herself against the far armrest. He wrapped his arms around her shoulders pulling her back into contact with him. She felt the heat of his shoulder, hip, and knee pressing against hers. The aroma of dust and desert and his manhood enveloped her.

Staring across the room and thinking about what Li'l Meg had said, she heard the Eleggua chant in her head. The chant that ended, "May the owner of gossip not lead me astray." She took a deep breath and tried to ignore the challenge of Master Clint's touch.

"Will the new tribute feed your children," she asked, "or will it go… elsewhere?"

A deathly silence filled the trailer. When Li'l Meg dropped her eyes, Marne knew the answer to her question.

"No one in Babapupa is starving," she said, drawing out her words. She tried to find of a diplomatic way of continuing, but could not. "No one is starving," she said, "because we don't steal from each other."

Master Clint stiffened and the threat of violence tightened the muscles of his arm.

She let the ugly truth envelop the room while preparing herself to receive whatever punishment he might inflict on her.

Neither Master Clint nor Li'l Meg responded to her provocation.

"You can take me home now," Marne said into the silence. "I will tell Akande, Malik and the rest of the council what I've seen. That's why Master Duke wanted you to show me your young people training, wasn't it?"

Both the father and the daughter remained silent, apparently unwilling to admit the truth of what she was saying.

"I don't know if my people will prefer the quick death of war over slow starvation," Marne continued. "We're dead either way."

The council wouldn't listen. Malik had discounted her vision and refused to share it with the rest of the others. The only hope of Verdant Valley, of the whole of the Babapupa Reserve, was the Sisterhood. Those were the ones she needed to tell about the empty eyes of the children in the encampment. Perhaps by the time she returned, the women would have found their own third way to save their people from these Demon Spawn.

Without waiting for a reply from either Master Clint or Li'l Meg, Marne stood up and walked to the rear of the trailer. She jammed her few things into the bag she had brought with her from her granny's, then set it by the door. Instead of returning to the sitting room, she went out. When he came looking for her, she would be on the front stairs. She needed someone's help getting home. Even if she took a cycle, she didn't know how to ride it, nor the way to Verdant Valley.

She looked around and soon found three stones the size of a man's fist. She piled them together on the left side of the stairway. Then she picked up five more rocks and balanced them into a pyramid on the right. Master Clint and Li'l Meg were arguing inside. It calmed her to build these small shrines to Eleggua the trickster on the left, and Oshun the patron of female artfulness on the right.

Perched on the step, she tried to calm herself. She hadn't been there long when a woman with two children walked by and waved at her. Waving back, she stood up and went toward them. Had they been among the little ones she had encountered earlier? The woman released the little girl who ran squealing to her. Marne caught her in her arms and swung her around, making her laugh.

She set the child down, then led her back to where her mother was waiting with a toddler the age of Kara, Anana's son. Like most of the women Marne had seen, she had a haggard, washed-out look, but she smiled.

"Are you Clint's new old lady?" she asked.

"Old lady?" Marne wasn't sure what she was asking. She felt as if she had aged in the short time she had been among the Demon Spawn, but was surprised it showed.

"His hag," the woman said, "his girlfriend?"

The question startled Marne. What was her relationship to Master Clint? She had not come to this camp willingly, but she had spent the night in his bed. She thought that had been to save herself from a more violent experience. Master Duke told him to take her back to her own people. But even after the things she'd just said she realized she wasn't sure that he would let her return. Had he claimed her according to an unknown Demon Spawn custom?

"I-I don't know," she said. "I don't think so. I think he's taking me home." At least I hope he is, she thought.

"Be careful," the woman said, gathering her children into her arms as though to protect them from some taint Marne carried from Master Clint's trailer. "He's very dangerous."

"Yes." She wanted to ask the woman more of her life in the encampment, how the women here allowed their men to starve their babies, but she heard the trailer door open behind her.

"Can you get to Verdant Valley?" Marne asked.

The woman nodded.

"Come and visit me," Marne said, tussling the younger child's hair. "My granny would love to fatten up your little ones."

The woman's eyes widened as someone grabbed Marne's arm and yanked.

"Get in here," Master Clint's voice commanded her.

Marne turned away from the woman. "Are you still mad at me?" she said, trying to decide where she stood with him.

"You can't be out there," he replied.

"Why? Did you think I'd run away?" she asked, widening her eyes to appear more innocent than she felt. "Where would I go? Or are you afraid of your own people?"

Instead of answering her questions, he grabbed her hand and pulled her up the stairs and into the trailer.

He kicked her bag. "What's this?"

"I'm ready to go home," she replied.

"You're not goin' anywhere." His voice was hard, cold as a winter dawn. She saw that he was still angry.

She pushed on. "Master Duke said you should take me back after you showed me what you called the pits," she told him. "I've seen it and I understand what he wants me to tell the council."

"You belong to me," Master Clint said, anger reddening his face again. "This is your home now."

"No," she said, "Master Duke told you to return me to my home. You can't keep me here."

"Clint," Li'l Meg interrupted their argument. "There are things you need to finish at Verdant Valley. You can't compromise Duke's plan." She gave her father a hard stare. "Let me take her. I'll see that she makes her report and leaves before they come for the tribute."

The woman didn't know that the Sisterhood was making their own plans for dealing with the Demon Spawn. Did she think Granny and the other women of Verdant Valley would let her bring Marne back here to live with Master Clint? Marne hoped she was wrong.

Li'l Meg turned to her. "You can leave your things here. We won't be gone that long. If we start now, I'll get you there before first light," she said. "I can make Malik call a meeting of the council. Then you tell them what you've seen." She turned back toward her father. "Do what you need to do to take our tribute. When you come home, she'll be here waiting for you."

"No," he said. "You haven't eaten since last night, and neither has she. You could ride through the night, but she can't. Wait and leave in the morning."

Marne saw the hungry look in Master Clint's eyes. He wasn't worried about her. She had avoided his lust all day, but her time of reckoning was coming. Could she play Oshun again? Maybe, but she could not stay on Li'l Meg's cycle after two nights with little or no rest.

"Wait," Marne said. "Master Clint's right. I'm famished. If we leave now, I'm not sure I can hold on all the way to Verdant Valley." She plopped down at the table to emphasize her exhaustion. "Let me sleep with you," she looked at Li'l Meg, "or alone out here. Then we can go first thing tomorrow."

Although she was looking at his daughter, she saw Master Clint frowning at her. He wasn't ready for her to return home and she was sure he did not want to go to bed by himself. But she could not play with him through the night and then ride back to Verdant Valley in the morning. He said nothing, so perhaps he agreed with what she said.

Silence hung in the air. Then Li'l Meg came into the cooking area, and started pulling out containers, pots, and pans. Marne stood up to help.

"Come here, darlin'," Master Clint called to her, patting the sofa next to him. His anger had softened into need.

Marne shook her head, reluctant to go to him.

"Get over here," his voice was low, its tone menacing.

When she was close, he pulled her onto his lap. Soon he covered her mouth with his and pushed her palm toward the bulge that had reappeared in his jeans.

"What have you done to me, darlin'?" he moaned when she cupped him. "Are you a witch?" His hand snaked under her tee shirt and pinched one nipple. She tried unsuccessfully to hold back her own groan.

Taking a deep breath, she attempted to regain her composure. She pushed away from him. "You brought me here and I've given you what you wanted," she whispered, resisting his pull. "I can't give you any more." He growled but let her move beside him on the sofa where he continued to caress her face and fondle her through her shirt.

Dinner was a silent affair. Marne kept Li'l Meg between herself and Master Clint as they got through the meal. When they moved to the sitting area, she stayed at the table. Before he forced her onto his lap, she walked to the rear of the trailer. She considered locking herself in Master Clint's room, but decided instead to duck into Li'l Meg's sleeping room.

She could not see the size and shape of the space so she slid down the wall next to the door. Sitting on the floor she began to weep. Ever since she had arrived at the encampment, she had tried to maintain her composure. She did not want him to know how frightened she was. But now, alone in the dark, she collapsed into a puddle of fear and loathing for Master Clint, Li'l Meg, and the rest of the Demon Spawn. She wept for things she had seen and done. She was afraid she could not release the control she had exerted over her captor. Maybe he would never let her return home to Verdant Valley and her life there.

She had cried herself out by the time she heard footsteps in the hallway. Someone opened the door of the other sleeping room.

"Are you waiting for me, darlin'?" Master Clint's voice wafted down the hall. "What the..." he said. "Where is she?"

Marne bit the back of her hand so no noise escaped from her. She listened to him pounding through his sleeping room and its attached bathing room looking for her.

She followed the sound of his steps as he slammed open the rear door. "Come back here, darlin'," he yelled into the night. The door shut and his voice disappeared.

She jumped when the door next to her opened and light flooded the space. Li'l Meg's space was smaller than Master Clint's but where his was tidy and masculine, hers was a mess of bedding and clothing.

"Oh, there you are," Li'l Meg said. She backed away and went to the rear or the trailer.

"Clint, Clint," she called. "I found her. Clint?"

The door shut behind her, leaving Marne alone as the two Demon Spawn searched for each other. She ran into the cooking room and filled a glass full of fresh water. Perhaps she could cool Master Clint's passion for her.

"… hiding," Li'l Meg was saying as the rear door opened and she led her father inside. Marne heard someone open the door to Li'l Meg's sleeping room. "Now where is she?" the woman said. "Look in your room. She's got to be here somewhere."

She waited for them to make their way to the front of the trailer.

"Here she is," Li'l Meg called out when she saw Marne sitting again at the table, the glass of water in front of her. "Clint! She's here."

The rear door slammed and Master Clint stomped along the hallway.

"Where have you been?" he demanded, looming over her. She read anger and something else in his face. Had he been worried about her?

She held out the glass to him. He stared at her. "What's this?" he asked.

"Cool water," she said, looking up at him. "It will make you feel better."

He swatted at the glass, but she pulled it back before he could knock it out of her hand. She looked away. How was she going to break the spell of his desire?

Li'l Meg came and sat beside her. "Why were you hiding?" she asked, her voice stern but not angry.

"I-I just want to go home," Marne said, tears leaking out of her eyes. "Please take me back." She took a sip of the water and then held it toward Master Clint again.

"This is your home now," the woman said wrapping her arm around Marne. "I'll take you back, but if your village council keeps defying us, Duke's forces will destroy Verdant Valley. Soon there won't be anywhere else for you to go."

Master Clint sat on the other side of her. He reached up and brushed her tears away. His touch was gentle although anger still clouded his forehead. She wrapped her hands around the water, humming the chant her granny used to dismiss an Orisha who didn't want to leave at the end of a ritual. Then she pushed the glass back toward him. Absently, he took it, gulping the contents in a couple swallows.

Marne watched his anger wane. Then his expression changed, his eyes cleared, and she could tell the obsession she had cultivated was fading away, too.

"Wh-what," he frowned. He blinked like a medium who had been caught too long in possession.

"Meg," he said finally, "get a blanket for me. I can sleep out here tonight and let our young guest have the back bedroom."

She looked from Marne to her father. "Did you do that?"

Marne nodded. Li'l Meg smiled. "You are a witch," she said.

CHAPTER 12

The journey to Verdant Valley was long but uneventful. Li'l Meg bypassed the turnoff to Marne's granny's workshop and instead took them into town and straight to the *obanla's* compound. After they dismounted, she pressed her hand into Marne's back and marched her through to Malik's offices and into his private sitting room.

"What...?" The *obanla* looked up as Li'l Meg pushed the door open.

"I tried to stop them, Sir," his assistant, Stephen, said from behind them.

"Call a meeting of the council," the Spawn woman commanded, ignoring both the assistant and any niceties. "This one has something to tell you."

"B-but..." Malik stuttered.

"Call a meeting. Now." Li'l Meg glared at the *obanla*.

"Stephen," Malik said, "do as the, ah, lady, asks." He turned back to Marne and Li'l Meg. "This will take a few minutes. Do you want to clean up or something?"

Marne nodded, eager to escape the Spawn woman.

"No," Li'l Meg responded. "We'll wait there. Bring a coffee for your girl and a beer for me. Oh, and something to eat." She pushed Marne into the *obanla's* sitting room. "Come get us when you're ready," she called over her shoulder and slammed the door behind them.

After the food and drink had been delivered, and they were alone again, Li'l Meg turned to Marne. "We need to talk about what you did to my father. But first, you will tell these people to quit trying to double-cross us." She gave Marne a stern look reminiscent of the one Master Duke had given her less than a day earlier. "Duke doesn't think your people can put up much of a fight, but it would be better for everyone if you give us what we ask for. Do you understand?"

Marne nodded. She'd been considering what to tell the council. Li'l Meg would be there to watch her performance, of course. Master Clint might show up, too. He'd been pretending to still be asleep when they left the trailer before dawn, but Marne doubted he would let his daughter handle this mission on her own.

She knew she needed to be convincing, but nothing she could say would deter Malik and the council. The *obanla* had already discounted her vision at the Market Board. However, the faster she finished here the sooner she could escape from the Spawn woman and return to her granny's workshop. She wanted to talk to her granny, find out what the Sisterhood might have planned, and share what she had seen among the women and children of the Demon Spawn.

Li'l Meg took a deep drink. "Mmm," she purred. "You people have the best beer. Maybe next year I'll convince Duke to add beer and coffee to the tribute."

Marne was surprised she didn't realize that there would be no further tributes after their demands destroyed the Reserve.

Li'l Meg looked at her captive. "Now, tell me what you did to Clint. How did you put your spell on him?"

"I can't."

"Don't be coy," Li'l Meg replied. "I've known that man all my life and even my mother couldn't control him as well as you did. You bewitched him and I want to know how."

Marne shook her head. She herself had been partially entranced with the spirit of Oshun, the goddess of pleasure, and later the trickster Eleggua. She could not explain that to Li'l Meg. And she wasn't sure she wanted to share the secret of the Orisha with her. Before she could find the right words, Stephen returned and led them into the council chambers.

The council members, their assistants, and their Demon Spawn shadows were there. As Marne expected, Lola sat alone. She was Lola's only assistant and Li'l Meg was her shadow. Malik and Akande, whom Master Clint and Master Duke shadowed, had new people standing behind them. Despite everything that happened at the encampment, she realized she had only been gone from Verdant Valley for a couple days.

Just as the *obanla* was calling the meeting to order, the door slammed open and Master Clint stomped in. Everyone in the room, villagers and shadows alike, shrunk into their chairs. He glanced around before taking a position opposite where Marne was standing next to the *obanla*. Her heart fell to the bottom of her belly. Had he come back to reclaim her or had she broken his fascination with her? He did not imply that there was, or had been, a special tie between them.

Malik looked from Master Clint to Li'l Meg to Marne, but no one spoke. Then, Marne stepped forward. She glanced away from Duke's people scattered around the room and toward Lola who smiled at her. She realized that Granny must have told her about Marne's abduction. Then she realized everyone knew. She didn't need to explain her absence.

She took a deep breath. "I've been to the Demon Spawn encampment. Master Clint showed me the preparations their young people are making in the event we try to defy them. I saw there is no way we can defeat their forces. They will slaughter our fighters. If we don't give them what they want, they will kill all of us."

There, she'd said it as clearly as she was able. She had planned on telling them the story of her visit to what Master Clint called the pits and the battle she had seen. However, when the time came, she couldn't bear to relive that. She'd told what Master Duke wanted them to know. Maybe now Master Clint and Li'l Meg would let her go.

The room buzzed as though she had released a hive of bees. Malik pounded his stick of power on the floor until the council came back to order. One at a time, members questioned her until she told the entire story again. She didn't tell them about the starving women and children or her conversation with the woman she had met the previous night. That part she was saving for the Sisterhood. She doubted Master Clint wanted them to know he and the other Spawn leaders abused their people. And she didn't want him to know she had invited the woman to come to Verdant Valley.

When she'd answered their questions, she took her place behind Lola, resuming her position as the Market Board representative's assistant. Master Clint continued to ignore her. However, Li'l Meg stared at her as Malik groveled and the rest of the council assured them that there was no plan to defy the Demon Spawn. They told him their tribute would be ready at the required time.

She saw the council's protests did not convince him. She realized there was a plan afoot and that the people of the village thought they could defeat the gang. As Marne had grasped before she'd left the encampment, there was nothing she could do or say to the council that would change the inevitable battle to come.

As soon as the meeting ended, Marne wanted to escape to her office. After conferring with Lola, Li'l Meg led the girl to the motorcycle. Was Li'l Meg going to force her back to the encampment before she checked on her granny or her sister? Hadn't Li'l Meg seen that Master Clint was no longer obsessed with her? Why couldn't they leave her alone?

Li'l Meg handed her the helmet and they climbed back onto the cycle. They rode to Marne's father's compound and parked in front of his apartment. Home. Li'l Meg had brought her home. As Marne dismounted, the Spawn woman grabbed her arm and gave her the black bag.

"Lola and I decided you are to stay at your grandmother's workshop. Get what you need. I'll be out here waiting." She glared at Marne. "Don't try anything and no one here will be hurt." She fingered the gun at her hip.

Marne nodded. She realized in that moment she had freed herself from the father but not the daughter.

Her father's apartment was empty. Marne wanted to have to talk to Perla, her younger sister, but everyone was gone. She filled the bag with the clean clothing and personal items she wished she had taken to the encampment. She drafted a long note to her sister and left it on their private network.

Then she went into the girls' small shrine room. It was more the size of a closet, but it was big enough for altars to both her patron, Yemaya, and Perla's Obatala. Collapsing before Yemaya and shaking the goddess's rattle, she poured out her heart. She asked the Great Mother for the strength and the wisdom she needed to walk the path before her.

She was basking in the soft love of her Orisha when she heard the front door of the apartment slam open. With one final prayer, she went to meet the Demon Spawn, pulling the door to the shrine room closed behind her.

"I'm ready." Marne picked up the bag and followed Li'l Meg back to the motorcycle. The compound courtyard was eerily empty. No children played under the watchful gaze of their mothers or babysitters. But Marne was sure there were many eyes watching her and the Demon Spawn from behind the curtained windows. The family saw what was happening even if they didn't make a move to stop the Spawn woman from taking her away again.

When she and Li'l Meg arrived at her granny's workshop, Marne fell into Gladys's arms. She was relieved both that the older woman looked well and that she had finally found a welcoming presence. Granny gave her a hug, favoring the arm Master Clint had broken mere days ago.

"I'll return later," Li'l Meg scowled. "We still need to talk. Do you understand?"

Marne nodded, and then she turned her back on the Demon Spawn and walked with her granny into the small house.

With coffee and tears, she told her granny the whole story of her time at the encampment, including her seduction of Master Clint and their visit to the pits.

"I tried to use the third way, like you taught me," she explained. "And it worked, maybe too well. I beguiled the father and gave the daughter some of the mother's love she needs. Now they want me to return with them."

Marne told her about the small shrine she'd built in front of Master Clint's trailer. She described the women and children she met as they walked through the encampment and the one family she invited to Verdant Valley.

"That woman and her babies were so weak. Li'l Meg confessed that Master Duke sold our tribute instead of giving it to his people. She said her own mother died because she was trying to carry a child without enough food."

Her granny's scowl deepened as Marne brought her story to a close.

"Master Duke wanted me to tell the council they could not defy him. But I don't think the *obanla* and Hackett, the leader of the Hunters Guild, were convinced."

Her granny nodded. The women of the Sisterhood knew what was happening out in the forests. It was only a secret from the gang and not a well-kept secret at that.

"There are many more of that gang than Hackett and Malik have seen," Marne told her. "With their guns and other weapons, they will be an overpowering force." She paused, still digesting what she had learned. "But the Demon Spawn are delusional, too. Li'l Meg thinks they can take their increased tribute and come back next year for more. But according to Talé, if we give them what they want, most of us wouldn't survive the winter. There won't be a Verdant Valley next year, and no more tribute."

Granny nodded, then put her good arm around Marne and pulled her against her. All Marne wanted to do was to lose herself in the softness of her granny, forgetting the Demon Spawn and their demands, leaving Master Clint and his daughter to themselves, to live or die as they chose.

"Baby, I can see you're exhausted," Granny said. "You're safe here, at least for a while. Go to the back and rest. Take the small room." She pushed Marne away so she could look her in the eye. "You must be brave and tell your story one more time when the Sisterhood meets tonight. Then we'll work together to find a third way out of this mess."

CHAPTER 13

Just as the moon was rising, the women began to arrive at Granny's tiny home. The first were Anana and Jumoke, Marne's godmother. As the former head of the Market Board Jumoke knew as well as anyone what the Demon Spawn tribute meant, not only to the people of Verdant Valley but also for the entire Babapupa Reserve. She was followed by Talé, who managed their largest and most prosperous farm. The last time Marne met with the Sisterhood, Talé had talked about arranging contributions from the other farmers to meet the gang's demands. She hadn't been optimistic then, and Marne wondered whether Talé's optimism had increased over the several days she had been gone.

Last to arrive was Lola along with Li'l Meg, who was back to shadowing her everywhere. How could the Sisterhood make plans with the Spawn woman in their midst? At least the councilwoman had convinced the Spawn woman to come without her guns and ammunition. Her scowl made her intimidating enough.

Granny greeted each woman, even Li'l Meg, with a quick hug and a peck on each cheek before leading them into her sitting room, where seven chairs waited for them. As they got settled, Marne brought in pots of tea, mugs, and trays of nibbles. Her granny had pulled a small table to the middle of the circle and set an indigo-blue pot inscribed with a crescent moon. There was also a natural wax candle and a bowl of water.

Jumoke picked up the water and carried it to the front door. They could hear her chanting: "*Omi Tutu, Ona Tutu, Ani Tutu, Ile Tutu, Egun Tutu, Laroye Tutu, Aiku Baba Wa.*" May cool water bless you. May a cool road lead you. May cool relatives surround you. May a cool house envelop you. May cool Ancestors watch over you. May the owner of gossip never lead you astray. May the ancestors bring their blessings to you. Then she clicked the lock shut and called out, "*Ashé.*"

As the youngest person in the room, Marne stepped forward and lit the candle. "*Ashé*," she mumbled. The women surrounding her answered with their own "*Ashé*."

There was a moment of silence as Jumoke set the bowl of water back on the table, then returned to her seat.

"Everyone has heard one version or another of our sister Marne's abduction and return," Lola said, "but I want you to hear it from her own mouth."

Marne looked to where Li'l Meg sat next to the councilwoman. She had expected to tell these women everything that had happened to her but was surprised that they included the Demon Spawn woman. What would she think of Marne's view of those events including the portions she'd left out of her report to the Council?

"Don't worry, dear," Lola said following Marne's eyes. "Our visitor says she knows the story. Do not insult her by holding back or sugarcoating the truth."

Marne wondered what to say about Akande and her first encounter with Master Clint but decided to begin with her abduction. If Lola felt her earlier incident was important, she could bring it up.

Once again she described her adventure. This time she told them of her conversation with Li'l Meg, and the women and children she met at the encampment.

"I discovered the leaders of the Demon Spawn are stealing from their own people," she said. "There are people in the encampment who are starving so Master Duke and his council can sell our tribute elsewhere."

She ended by telling them of meeting the woman and her two children and her invitation for them to come visit Verdant Valley.

"I don't know if we have enough to feed all those hungry Demon Spawn," Marne said, "but…" She let the resolution hang in the air.

She watched Li'l Meg as she talked. She could tell the woman wanted to hide her feelings as Marne told her story, but her expression said everything. She was embarrassed when Marne revealed their private conversation, and proud when she described the pit and the battle she observed. She seemed surprised to hear Marne tell the Sisterhood she had invited one of her people to Verdant Valley. She had not mentioned that to anybody. She wondered how Master Duke and Master Clint and the others described the Reserve. It was obvious they thought the people of Babapupa were so rich they could easily give up their harvest to the Demon Spawn.

No one spoke after Marne finished. The sounds were of tea being poured into cups and platters of nibbles being passed around the room. Once everyone considered what she had told them, the women turned toward Li'l Meg.

"Is it true, what our sister said?" Lola asked. "Are your leaders letting the little ones go hungry?"

Li'l Meg looked at Marne with defiance. "That one talks too much," she hissed.

"I can see she does," Jumoke said, her voice soothing. She reached out to lay her hand on Li'l Meg's arm, but the woman shook her off.

"She was supposed to tell you about Duke's army. No more." She continued to stare at Marne, ignoring the other women in the room. "You may have bewitched my father, but you can't stop Duke. He takes what he wants. And what he wants from you," Li'l Meg looked around, "from all of you, is that tribute. What he does with it is none of your concern." She gazed away from the women and toward a spot far away. "The weak must support the strong for the good of the whole." She spoke in the singsong manner of a group chant.

Then Li'l Meg's facade crumbled and a single tear crept out of her eye and made its slow way down her cheek. "Yes," she whispered. "Everything she said is true. Our fighters are well-trained and well-fed. Many others are not. Our men are prepared to die in battle. Some women and children will die, too." She straightened her shoulders as if stating an obvious fact. "Those who survive are making us stronger." Then she collapsed into herself again.

Jumoke put her arm around the woman's shoulders and pulled her into her ample bosom. Granny began her quiet chanting. "*Pinkun! Pinkun! Ajanbiti!* We are *Iyami*, we are the mothers." The other women joined in, keeping their voices to a whisper as the Demon Spawn wept. Marne thought she cried for her mother and the brother or sister that had died in her mother's womb, but perhaps there were others she loved who had died.

When Li'l Meg appeared to have cried herself out, the chanting faded to silence. She tried to sit up, but Jumoke put her hand on the back of the *oyinbo* head's and the Spawn relaxed into her.

"I've heard Master Clint and the others talk," Lola said. "They think we are rich because even in the worst times we don't abandon our weakest members. They believe if everyone has enough we must have hidden stores to draw on."

Talé nodded in agreement. Because she had arranged the earlier tributes, she had more contact with the Demon Spawn than the rest of the women. "They don't understand taking this tribute will destroy us, destroy the whole Reserve. Some of them are talking about what added goods they will demand next year." She shook her head. "If we give them everything they are demanding, there won't be a next year."

Lola caught each woman's eye in turn. When she looked at the *oyinbo*, she was sitting up again. Her arms were wrapped around her middle as though her pain had settled deep in her belly. Her eyes were bloodshot and watery and her pale face was splotchy red and white, but she had stopped crying.

"We've come together tonight as the Sisterhood of the Moon," Lola said. "Verdant Valley stands at a crossroad and now it seems the Demon Spawn, too, are at a crossroad. The road forward is full of blood and violence. No one wins such a struggle."

"*Ashé, o,*" Jumoke agreed using the ritual language. "And we think we can find a third way. A way that allows everyone to survive."

"We have been six, the number of balance but also the number of conflict," Granny said. "Now we want to become seven. We have learned more about our adversary, the Demon Spawn. Now we want to make common cause against the forces ranged against us and our children."

Talé looked around the room as though asking for permission from the other women. Several nodded. "Tonight we are looking for a third way that will preserve both the people of Verdant Valley and Meg's Demon Spawn. Tonight we invite Meg to join with us, to join our Sisterhood, to help find a solution to the impending crisis."

After a long silence, Lola said, "Meg, will you join us? Will you become our sister at this dangerous time?"

Conflicting emotions flitted across Meg's face. Surprise, then fear, then a kind of hope as the final pieces of her armor against them fell away. She nodded.

"Yes, yes," she stuttered. "I'll join your Sisterhood. But..." she pulled back. Then leaned forward. "No. No 'buts.' I'll join you to save your people and mine."

The room exploded as everyone rushed to embrace Meg as their newest sister. Only Marne held back. She wondered how Meg could be both their sister and Master Clint's daughter, a respected member of the Demon Spawn.

After everyone welcomed Meg into their sisterhood, the women returned to their seats. Marne refilled the teapot and replenishing the trays of nibbles. Getting Meg on their side had changed nothing. She hoped the other women had a plan in mind, a way out of this crisis.

"Before we can move ahead, we need to talk about how Meg is going to keep our secrets." As usual Talé cut straight to the center of the issue.

"Meg, we realize you now have divided loyalties." Marne's granny smiled at her. "You've agreed to be a part of us, but when you leave here tonight you'll still be a member of the Spawn." She held up her broken arm. "That scares me."

Meg stared at her, then nodded. "I don't know," she whispered. "Clint will want a report of everything that happened out here." She looked from one to the other and shook her head. "I watched your granddaughter manipulate my father, so you may be able to do what you want to do. But Clint knows me too well. I never could lie to him." She frowned. "I shouldn't be here." She stood. "Lola, I'll be back later to get you."

"Wait." Marne hadn't talked since telling her story, letting the mothers and grandmothers lead their meeting. She motioned Meg to sit.

"When I was at the encampment, I called on the Orisha to help me. Oshun helped me deal with Master Clint." She smiled. "Meg can tell you more about that if you're interested. But I also called on the spirit of Eleggua," she turned to Meg, "the trickster. We call him the 'owner of gossip.'" She turned back toward the group. "Like Eleggua, I tried to use the truth against Master Duke. I told him and Master Clint the Hunters Guild was gathering people together to fight his army. He thought the idea was ludicrous. Then I told him about our Sisterhood. He laughed harder to think of a bunch of market of women and artisans challenging him and his forces."

Everyone was staring at her and frowning. Marne wasn't sure whether they were angry because she gave away the secret of the Sisterhood to the Demon Spawn or because Master Duke had laughed at them.

Then Lola nodded. "'May the owner of gossip never lead you astray,'" she said, quoting their opening prayer. "Marne is right. If the Spawn have already discounted us, then it doesn't matter what Meg says. The more she tells them the truth, the more they will disregard it."

She turned to Meg. "Can you protect us by telling your father and the rest of your people the truth?"

Meg considered what Lola had said, then nodded. She looked at Marne. "You were right. Duke was suspicious of everything you said. Even when I told him about my visits out here, he thought you had fooled me. He and Clint know you people are planning something, but they won't believe what I tell them, especially about your Sisterhood. They assume all of you are liars, trying to deceive us at every turn."

She stared at Marne. "You bewitched my father and now I see you used trickery against Duke, too. We need to talk, little sister."

"Harrumph," Marne's granny snorted. "Don't your women know anything?"

Before Meg could respond, Lola interrupted, "If that's settled, then, it's time we discover our own third way."

Marne looked at Lola apologizing in advance for what she was going to say. "Before Master Clint abducted me, I had met with him in Akande's office. That night the head of the Traders Council called Master Clint his friend. Since returning I've noticed the two of them whispering together." She turned toward Meg. "Is it possible they are planning their own third way? Some defiance of Master Duke and his demands?"

Meg thought for a moment, then shook her head. "Clint is Duke's enforcer. He would never defy him. My father and I have enough because of Duke. He wouldn't endanger us like that."

Marne turned toward Lola, who also shook her head. "I can't imagine why Akande and Master Clint might whisper together. Perhaps my husband thinks there is a strategy for softening the Spawn's demands."

Meg snorted as though to say, You people are such fools.

When no one else spoke, Marne realized that nothing had changed while she was gone. The women were a willing group, but they had no idea of how to move forward.

Then Anana whispered, "We can't let their babies die."

The women turned toward her. "Marne said they were letting their woman and children starve to feed their fighters." Anana looked at Meg. "Is that true? Are your women and children dying because they don't have enough food?"

Meg nodded. "Not everyone is starving. Clint has always seen that we both had sufficient food. But many others go hungry so Duke can buy what he wants."

"I know nothing about fighting or the third way or how Meg will cloud her father's mind, or any of the things you're talking about," Anana stammered. "But I still have milk. Kara is mostly weaned but I still have milk. Maybe I could save their babies."

Everyone stared at Anana.

"Yemaya be praised," Jumoke cried. "The Great Mother speaks through one of her own."

"She's right." Talé's words were slow as she worked out the implication of what Anana had said. "She's right. Not only does she still have milk but we, Verdant Valley, still have food. We're not starving, not yet anyway."

"But that's the problem," Marne's granny argued. "If we send our food to the Demon Spawn, we will be the ones going hungry."

"And our newest sister said when we send food to the Spawn, they sell it instead of feeding their people," Lola replied. "I don't see where you're going with this."

Granny frowned. "Do we still have enough food to share with our sister Meg's sisters and their children?" She turned to Talé.

The farm manager nodded. "And as long as we have food, we can feed whoever we want. If we want to feed the women and children of the Demon Spawn, we can."

"But we can't send the food to them." Lola smiled as she finally got the point. "The only way to make sure they are fed is if they come to us."

Marne brewed more tea, brought out mugs of beer, and prepared more nibbles while the rest of the women worked out the logistics of their plan. At first Meg was reticent, not able to see the difference between the Sisterhood's proposal and the tribute Duke was demanding. When it finally dawned on her what the Sisterhood was planning, she smiled. Then she joined in helping refine and perfect their idea.

As Marne listened to the idea unfold, she wondered what Master Clint would think when Meg made her report on their meeting. She would tell him everything, of course. Would he be surprised at their audacity or would he discount it as the work of "market woman and artisans"? Either way, he would be amazed when the Sisterhood defied the Demon Spawn and succeeded. Because she felt they finally had a plan that would succeed.

CHAPTER 14

After everything that had happened, Marne was glad to settle back into the rhythm of her work for Lola and the village council. Her granny and Lola decided that Marne should return home to her father's compound and to her job at the *obanla's*. The Demon Spawn still infested the council offices monitoring them. Marne assumed they were trying to prevent the sort of defiance that the women and Hunters Guild were planning. She wondered whether there were other groups planning a rebellion.

The council's work continued unabated and Marne soon found herself immersed in the meetings and reports that were the normal part of her position. She hadn't returned from her adventures unscathed. She maintained a visceral awareness of both Akande and Master Clint as they moved through the offices. They were often together. She remembered Clint calling him his friend when he had first discovered her in his sitting room and wondered whether those two planned their own acts of defiance.

Although there was nothing overt, Marne felt both of the men continued their sinister surveillance of her. She was aware of their eyes following her as she went about her business. More disturbing was the way they watched her during the council meetings. Akande still smirked and winked at her when he thought Lola wouldn't notice. Marne worried that she'd never be free from his attentions.

Master Clint replaced his flirtatious manner with something more predatory. His unblinking stares reminded Marne of a snake stalking a songbird. He never approached her. He even tried to avoid passing her in the hallways. It was as though he both feared and coveted her. The other Demon Spawn also acted strange around her. Not deferential, but with an obsequiousness she found unnerving.

The staff acted peculiar, too. Everyone knew of Marne's abduction and return. But many of them seemed to think Master Clint still had a hold over her, or that she had some influence over him. Perhaps, she thought, she did have some residual effect on the man. It appeared that her attempt to break the connection between them had not been completely successful.

Together Lola and Meg arranged it so that Marne was seldom alone in the *obanla's* compound. If she had to work late, the Spawn woman sat at the other desk, watching as if Lola's assistant was the most subversive of the staff members. Either Lola or Meg escorted her home at the end of the day. There was no opportunity for any after-hours mischief by Akande, Master Clint, or anyone else. When Meg was her escort, she often stayed for a beer and to share the evening meal with Marne and her sister.

In the days that followed, the three women developed a different relationship. Although Meg continued to wear the intimidating guns and bandoliers of the Spawn, she moved with a new grace. Joining the Sisterhood seemed to make her more at ease with herself and her place in the world. As the women had discussed, she told Master Clint about her meeting with them and their plans to thwart the demands of the Spawn. As expected, he had laughed and ridiculed them, dismissing any possibility of success.

Although Meg was assigned to Lola, she overnighted so often with Marne that she began to move her few possessions into the apartment. No one questioned the change, but it gave the two young women opportunities to learn more about each other. In many ways, Meg, who was around five years older than Marne, became the sister she and Perla wished they'd had. Marne thought the Spawn woman enjoyed their time together, too. Meg was very curious about the Orisha and how she had used their power at the encampment. Marne explained as well as she could. However, if Meg wanted to know more, she needed to go out to the shrines. There she could get a divination and a formal introduction to the world of the deities.

Late one day as the work of the council members and their staff was winding down, Marne heard a commotion out in the halls.

"Clint's old lady. Where is she?" a shrill voice demanded.

Marne followed Meg out the door and through the hall to the front reception room. She didn't recognize the woman with the two little children she had met that night in the encampment. But the children remembered her, racing into her arms.

"What are you doing here, Kandy Lynn?" Meg hissed, grabbing the woman's arm and pulling her toward the offices.

Marne picked up the children and followed Meg and their mother into the back office space. They were filthy, as was their mother. It was a long, dirty ride from the encampment to Verdant Valley. But from what Marne could see of both the mother and the children, their grime was more deep-seated.

Meg pushed open the door to Lola's sitting room. Since Lola had left for the day, it was a good place for a private conversation.

Marne deposited the children on a sofa and went to the sideboard where the councilwoman kept a pitcher of cool water and coffee above and beer below. She poured water for the children, then pulled out beers for herself and the two Spawn women.

Meg glared at the newcomer. "What are you doing here?" she asked again.

Kandy Lynn looked from her to Marne, then back again. "She told me," she said, nodding toward Marne. "I know she's Clint's hag and when she invited me, I decided to come."

Meg scowled at Marne.

"It's part of our plan," Marne smiled, then reached over and tickled the children who giggled and squirmed.

"She said they had plenty to eat here, and the children were hungry." Kandy Lynn glanced at the beer cradled in her lap, then back up at Meg. "I know what Duke and them said. But she," the woman nodded toward Marne, "she said I should come. She wouldn't have done that without Clint's permission, would she?" The woman's voice dropped off, as though she realized she had made a grave mistake.

Marne put her finger to her lips, then said, "I'm not Master Clint's, what do you call it? His hag?" She shuddered to think she might not have completely cut her ties with Clint.

A sudden look of panic filled the woman's face.

"But," she continued, "I did invite you and I think you should come home with me," she looked at Meg, "with us. Our sisters will want to meet you." She stood up. "They can come to our apartment tonight. You two enjoy your beer while I finish up my work." She turned to the woman. "Then we'll have a nice meal and see what we can do."

Without giving Meg an opportunity to protest, Marne slipped out of the sitting room and back to her office. Before she shut down her display for the evening, she sent a message to Lola. "Please invite the Sisterhood to my apartment for dinner and conversation. Meg and I have a special guest we want our sisters to meet. The third way has launched."

Marne and Perla opened one of the spare sleeping rooms in the apartment. Since their father and his new wife had taken their own private quarters, there was more than enough space for Kandy Lynn and her children. They showed her to a room with its adjoining bathing area and suggested they get cleaned up while the girls made the evening meal. Perla scrounged up clothing for the children and donated a pair of jeans and a tee shirt for Kandy Lynn.

By the time the rest of the Sisterhood arrived, each with her own contribution toward the meal, both the children and Kandy Lynn herself had been scrubbed clean. She watched as pot after platter was set on the table for herself and her children. No one had been extravagant, so the food was simple but filling. Surrounded by so many new grannies, the exhausted children were soon fed. Perla took them to the back and put them to bed.

Gathered in the main sitting room with either mugs of tea or bottles of beer, the women studied Kandy Lynn. She was a mousy-looking woman with dark brown hair and sky-blue eyes. She sat on the sofa next to Jumoke, who pulled her close. Her earlier *bravado* was gone, replaced with a timid reticence.

"Tell us again what you are doing here, Kandy Lynn." Meg hadn't yet lost her scowl. Marne wondered why she was so angry. Wasn't this just what they had agreed to?

Jumoke hugged their visitor as though trying to soften Meg words.

"She invited me," Kandy Lynn said. "I thought she was Clint's old lady." She looked from one woman to the other. "She was right. You do have plenty of food here." She stared into her lap. "I shouldn't have come. Duke and Clint told us to stay away from here. I should have listened to them." She glanced back toward Meg. "Please don't tell them. Things are too hard already, what with Junior gone."

Meg softened. "Tell them about Junior," she said.

Kandy Lynn sat up straighter. "My Junior used to be our leader, when Duke was his number two. They did everything together, and we had all we needed. Then Junior and Duke went on that raid of one of the Republic strongholds and only Duke came back. He said Junior was killed or captured by the Rangers. I still don't know which." She frowned. "Now we have nothing. Duke has taken all we have to build up the fighters."

For a moment, Marne wondered about the relationship between the Rangers who enforced Republic law and the Spawn who appeared to be outlaws.

"Doesn't Master Duke take care of you and your children?" Jumoke asked.

Kandy Lynn shook her head. "Oh, no. Duke never liked me. He said I tried to make Junior too soft. Now he says we all must support the strong for the good of the whole."

"Duke's made lots of promises." Meg's anger at Kandy Lynn seeming redirected toward Duke. "Every raid is going to bring us back to the glory days of Junior." She shook her head. "Things have just gotten worse."

Kandy Lynn seemed to collapse into herself.

"Duke doesn't know you're here, does he?" Meg asked.

"Oh, no," Kandy Lynn said. "He'd kill me if he knew."

Meg nodded.

Marne at the other women. "Isn't this our plan?" she asked. "Don't we want Kandy Lynn and her sisters here?"

"Well, yes, that was what we agreed," Lola conceded, "but not so soon. We're not ready. We haven't gotten the agreement from the other compounds."

Silence enveloped the room.

"I can take her," Anana said. "We have the space and Kara would love having some older children to play with. Marne's already hosting Meg." She nodded, working out the logistics. "I'll tell the family Clint is making me. No one will ask him if that's true."

Marne's granny laughed. "You'll tell your family the Spawn is making you take in a fugitive from the Spawn?"

Anana agreed, "They don't know what is going on at the *obanla's compound*. Meg's Spawn and she's moved in with Marne. Why shouldn't I have my own Spawn?"

Laughter swirled around the room as each woman considered the implications of using the Spawn's known authoritarian behavior against them.

"Perhaps we should share our plans with our guest. She might not be so willing to stay with us once she knows what she's getting into," Lola said.

So the women explained their idea for dealing with the challenge facing them. It took a while for Kandy Lynn to understand what they meant by the third way. They explained how it could work to the benefit of both the people of Verdant Valley and the women and children of the Demon Spawn.

"We'll protect you as much as we can," Lola promised. "But someone needs to go back to your encampment and recruit more of your people."

"I could," Meg said, "however, I'm not sure how many of the weakest will trust me." She frowned. "I'm Clint's daughter, after all."

Kandy Lynn nodded. "I remember your mother," she said, "but since Duke's taken over, you've had the best of everything."

Meg nodded, shame coloring her face.

"After Kandy Lynn's rested, she and Meg can go back together," Lola said, "but you must tell the people they need to each come alone, not in groups. In the meantime, we'll arrange places for them with the compounds. Someone will meet them at Gladys's workshop and bring them into the village after dark. We don't want Duke and Clint knowing what we're doing. Not yet, anyway."

The women nodded. The plan was initiated.

CHAPTER 15

Marne led Meg toward Jumoke's family compound. When her new sister wanted to know more about what she called Marne's "witchcraft," she realized she needed to reveal more about her way of life. However, she soon was in over her head trying to answer Meg's questions. She wanted to know more than Marne was comfortable answering. How do you explain the entire foundation of a society to a complete outsider?

Meg wanted to dress in the black leather trousers and vest that appeared to be her normal costume. However, Marne persuaded her to change into a less intimidating shirt and denim pants. She also convinced Meg to leave her gun and its accessories behind. Unwilling to leave them unguarded in the apartment, Meg made a great show of locking everything away in the side case of her motorcycle.

Jumoke had been a senior priest at the Yemaya shrine since she was Anana's age. Marne hoped she would be willing to answer all of Meg's questions. As a widow, Jumoke had left her husband's compound and returned to that of her own family. She had a large, comfortable apartment complete with a huge shrine room where she worshipped Yemaya, her other Orisha, and her ancestors. She was also Marne's godmother, the one who led her into the worship of her primary Orisha, Yemaya. Marne and Jumoke spent many hours in her shrine room as Marne came into her role of priestess and speaker.

Neither Jumoke nor Marne suggested taking Meg out to the forest where there were shrines for all the Orisha. The woods were a sacred area not open to the *oyinbo* who visited Verdant Valley. The Hunters Guild were also training in those woods. Their activities may have become an open secret between the people of Verdant Valley and the Demon Spawn. However, Jumoke did not think it would be a good idea to take a gang member out there, even if she was a member of the Sisterhood. Meg could not reveal knowledge she did not know.

Now, when Marne and Meg knocked on the door to Jumoke's apartment, she didn't respond. Marne was surprised, since Jumoke was expecting them. She tried a different tack. This was a spiritual journey. Rapping again, she called out "*Ago*," the greeting in their ritual language.

Through the door a voice answered, "Who's there?"

"Marne Abelabu, and…" she looked at Meg. "What's your full name?"

"Maggie Sue Sapulpa," she called out.

"What do you want?" Jumoke's voice asked.

Marne looked her companion. How far was Meg willing to go on this quest? Were the Orisha calling her to be more than their sister in this time of crisis?

"We want to learn about the Orisha," Marne said. It was a neutral answer, not asking for more than Meg might be willing to undertake.

The door opened wide. Jumoke was dressed in ritual white with a pristine white head tie. Marne began to fall into the prostration such a ritual encounter demanded but Jumoke caught her and encircled her in a hug instead.

"*Ashé, O*," she said. Then she inspected Meg as though they had never met. When Meg held out her hand in the greeting of the *oyinbo*, Jumoke grabbed it and pulled her into a hug as well.

"Welcome, Sister," Jumoke said. "You are very brave." She led them into the sitting room where coffee and nibbles were set out.

"My goddaughter," Jumoke nodded toward Marne, "tells me you have questions." She smiled. "Outsiders like you," Marne noticed Jumoke did not use the more derogatory "*oyinbo*," "aren't usually interested in our sacred ways. Yet here you are, asking probing questions. Are you prepared for all the answers will bring?"

Meg stared at Jumoke for a long time. Marne could tell she was conflicted. She was curious about Marne's activities at the encampment and the mystical systems behind them. However, as Marne learned from their conversations, Meg also feared Marne's "magic." Marne had tried to tell her that the knowledge she was seeking might not be free.

Finally, Meg nodded. "Marne explained that there might be a cost." She pulled out an old-fashioned leather wallet. "I am prepared to pay."

"Put your money away, sweetie," Jumoke said, leaning forward. "Are you willing to pay a personal price? Are you willing to transform yourself?"

Again, Meg was silent. Marne understood her hesitation. When she had first gone to the Yemaya shrine, Marne knew she was supposed to be initiated into Yemaya's worship. However, she was so frightened she almost bolted before Jumoke could open the door and invite her in.

"I-I guess so." Meg threw her head back, revealing her uncertainty.

"We'll take it slow," Jumoke said. "I'll try not to ask for more than you are willing to give. But…" She let the conclusion of her promise hang in the air.

Jumoke picked up a mug of coffee and sat back in her chair. "Well, then, what has Marne told you already?"

With that Jumoke began the education of Li'l Meg, the Demon Spawn who was now one of their Sisterhood. Meg wanted to jump straight to what she called "Marne's magic," but Jumoke held her back.

"First, you must to learn about the Orisha in general," Jumoke said. "You need to understand their place in the invisible world and in ours, their numbers and colors, their wants and needs, their relationships with each other and with us."

Hours later, after Marne could see that Meg's head was swimming with a whole world she never knew existed, Jumoke turned to Marne and smiled.

"I think our friend is ready to meet the Orisha," she said.

"Take off your shoes," she told Meg, "then come with me." She walked away leaving Meg and Marne to follow.

Marne slipped off her own shoes, then waited as Meg unlaced her heavy boots. When they were both barefooted, Marne led her sister into the large sleeping room Jumoke had made into her shrine room.

Although larger and more extravagant than Marne's, Jumoke's shrine room wasn't that different. Opposite the entrance was a multi-tiered altar for her Orisha. Hidden in a massive, ice-blue ceramic pot, Yemaya, her primary deity, was installed at the highest point. Below were the pots of various sizes and colors that served as the residences of the other Orisha. The number of containers attested to the fact that Jumoke had served the Orisha for a lifetime.

On the left side of the room was a simpler display for her *egun*, her esteemed ancestors and spirit guides. The pots on that display were smaller and more modest than those on the main altar.

Flickering candles and dim lights added an air of mystery to the space. When they entered, Marne went to the front of the Yemaya altar and prostrated herself on the straw mat laid out there, as was expected.

"*A wa-wa-to, Yemaya.*" Jumoke touched Marne's shoulders. "*Oh-di-de.*" Marne stood and embraced her godmother. "*Ashé,*" she said, completing the ritual greeting of the Orisha and their priest.

Then Marne rolled the mat out of the way and motioned Meg forward to stand in front of the altar. Although Marne recognized each Orisha symbol and offering displayed, she knew how overwhelming it must appear to someone like Meg who had never seen such a thing before.

Jumoke pointed to the topmost pot. "This is Yemaya," she said. "The deity that owns my head, and Marne's. That yellow pot belongs to Oshun, whom you met in a certain way back at your encampment. Over here is Ogun, the blacksmith and owner of all weapons. He is the patron of our Hunters Guild." She pointed to the open cauldron that held Ogun's tools, including a collection of knives and machetes.

"And behind you, next to the door, is Eleggua, the trickster."

Meg turned back toward the entrance. Trying to view it all through Meg's eyes, Marne saw the small humanoid head fashioned from cement and cowrie shells. She wondered whether Meg realized the impressive power of that modest-looking Orisha. When Meg nodded, Marne suspected that she was beginning to understand the power of their deities.

Jumoke introduced Meg to the rest of the deities on the altar and explained the *egun* shrine. "Sit here," she said, leading Meg to a small table set off on the right side of the room. Jumoke was a gifted diviner. Marne had had many divination sessions and learned much about her path with the Orisha sitting in that very chair. Now Meg's curiosity would lead her from knowledge to experience. Marne wondered whether she was ready.

"The Orisha are not just mythical beings represented by these pots," Jumoke said. "They are living beings who can speak to us. Marne," she nodded toward her godchild, "has the special talent of being able to embody the Orisha and allow them to speak through her. You've seen a bit of that, I think."

Meg nodded, her eyes sparkling. Now, Marne thought, Meg expects to learn the secrets of their magic.

"But there is another way the Orisha can talk to us," Jumoke continued as though unaware of Meg's revived interest.

She paused, watching Meg's excitement build.

"You have questions that only the Orisha can answer," Jumoke continued.

Meg nodded. This was what she had come for.

"The Orisha often answer the question in our deepest heart and not the one we are asking. Are you prepared to hear the truth about yourself and your life?"

Watching this performance, Marne knew nothing would keep Meg from requesting the divination that could change her life. The Orisha were calling to her and she could no longer back away.

Fear flitted across Meg's face. She was beginning to realize the danger of going forward. Then she nodded as Marne knew she would.

Jumoke scrutinized her as if to ask, "Are you sure?"

When Meg nodded again, Jumoke said, "My goddaughter will show you to the bathing room. Wash your hands and face in cool water while I prepare. Now you will need to make a cash offering. Marne will help you with that, too. When you return, we will begin."

Meg stood up and followed Marne. No longer was she the bold member of the gang. Instead she was another seeker come to consult the Orisha.

When they returned to the shrine room, Jumoke had set up the table for a divination session. A straw mat and her divination tools covered the top of the table. Marne brought a gourd of water and set it beside the cowrie shells, chalk, and a small black stone. Jumoke pulled a chair next to hers. A portable display waited for Marne there. Her job would be to record the messages and instructions of the Orisha, so nothing would be forgotten.

Meg sat down and handed Jumoke the small wad of cash. Jumoke took the twenty-one Republic dollars and held them together with the cowries, the chalk, and the stone. Then she swirled everything together on the mat.

"*Omi Tutu, Ona Tutu, Ani Tutu, Ile Tutu, Egun Tutu, Laroye Tutu, Aiku Baba Wa,*" she intoned. May cool water bless you. May a cool road lead you. May cool relatives surround you. May a cool house envelop you. May cool Ancestors watch over you. May the owner of gossip never lead you astray. May the ancestors bring their blessings to you.

Meg's divination was begun. There would be no backing away now.

"Yemaya loves you very much," Jumoke said when the shells fell in the common seven-mouth-up position. Seven was Yemaya's sacred number and Marne knew she spoke very strongly in any session that began in this way. She wasn't surprised that Yemaya was the first to speak to Meg. She still grieved for her own mother and suspected it was that grief that led Meg to join their Sisterhood. Issues of family relationships and one's personal destiny were also important when the shells fell with seven mouths up. Jumoke would not spare their guest as she moved forward. Meg had come to find out more about the villagers and the Orisha, but she would leave knowing much more about herself.

"Tell me about your mother," Jumoke said. "Is she still alive or dead?"

Meg looked stricken. She had not expected things to get so personal so quickly. Meg told Jumoke the same story of her mother's death she had told Marne. She began with a stoic recitation of the facts, but Jumoke's probing soon had tears streaming down her face. Meg not only described her mother's story but also unleashed the emotions she was hiding behind her stony facade. She filled the shrine room with her feelings of loss, guilt, fault, and melancholy.

"We believe our family never abandons us," Jumoke said. "I feel as though your mother is here with us now. What would you like to tell her?"

Another wave of grief seemed to engulf Meg. She began to say all those things she wished she had told her mother before she died and all that had transpired since.

During Meg's outpouring of grief, Marne and Jumoke learned much about the recent history of the gang. Their activities before and after Duke became their leader. The corruption of their own moral codes, which were rather loose by Babapupa standards. There was drought and hunger everywhere in the Republic of the Great American Southwest. But the gang as led by Duke and his inner circle had been especially hard-hit. Many of their gang, including Meg's mother, died because of their leaders' double-dealing.

Marne handed her a cloth to wipe away her tears and regain her composure. But Jumoke was not finished.

"We will need to deal with your mourning," Jumoke said as Meg finished. "What about your father? What is your relationship?"

Meg pushed herself into her chair as though she was about to refuse to continue with the session. Marne felt sorry for her. She had had to face many of these same questions when Jumoke first agreed to lead her into the priesthood. She had heard much of Meg's story earlier, but in this moment she was struck by how similar her own story was to Meg's.

"At first I thought my father didn't care that Mom died and left us alone. He buried her with no fanfare, dry-eyed and remorseless. But now I realize I was wrong," Meg said. "He was devastated, but the only feeling he showed was anger. I have always blamed Duke for Mother's death, but it wasn't long afterwards he recruited Clint as his enforcer. When we joined the top dogs, I buried my pain and so did Clint." Tears returned to her eyes. "Duke used Clint's anger for his own purposes. My father was never a nice man, but when he became Duke's enforcer, he became a real brute."

She turned to Marne. "I still don't know how you tamed him," she said. "He and Mom always had an explosive relationship, but you opened something else in him. I wish you would come back with me."

Marne shook her head. She never wanted to see Master Clint again and would never willingly return to his trailer.

Before Meg could draw Marne back into her life, Jumoke picked up the shells and swirled them on the mat again.

She let them fall. "*Irosun*," she said. Four mouths up this time.

Marne noted the completed throw, seven-four, *Odi-Irosun*. She wondered where Jumoke would take Meg's divination now. Each number had its own proverb and story, and each combination also had stories and proverbs. The proverb most commonly associated with seven was "Where the grave was first dug." The corresponding story told of a time when bodies were not buried but carried deep into the woods. That practice changed when someone pretended to die to learn what his family and friends said about him. After he returned to confront them, the people buried their dead to prevent future such resurrections.

Jumoke's probing revealed Meg's own experience of death and its after-effects, but now four mouths-up had fallen. Now, the divination would look toward Meg's future.

"What do you need to live?" Jumoke asked. This was the standard question when *Odi-Irosun* faced them, but Meg seemed taken back at the change of tone. It was typical when asked this question for people to name all the physical things they needed and desired. Talk of food, water, clothing, and shelter slipped out. The diviner had to be patient to get to the person's deeper needs.

As expected, Meg began by naming the needs that first brought her and her gang to Verdant Valley. The need for food, for the Republic dollars that food could bring in the City, and for the things that money could buy. As part of Duke's inner circle, she and Clint no longer went hungry, but Meg watched Duke's other cronies. Soon she wanted everything they had, fine new cycles, trailers. The best weapons and training. New clothes and all the markings of the leaders of their cutthroat society.

When she ran down, Jumoke nodded and asked, "What else?"

Meg's quizzical look told Marne that she had not thought beyond the things she could acquire. But Jumoke was wiser.

"You're a strong and beautiful young woman," Jumoke said. "Surely you want more than that. Did Duke send you here because you're Clint's daughter? Or did you bring other gifts? Don't you have your own ambitions?" She paused as if thinking. "Perhaps there is a young man that's caught your eye. Are you looking to have your own mate, your own children?" She paused again. "And why did you come to me? What are you looking for here? I don't think it's only curiosity. Why are you really here?"

At the mention of a mate and children, Meg's hand slipped to her belly in the unconscious movement Marne associated with newly pregnant women. Had Meg revealed a woman's most precious secret to them? And who might be the father of this child? Marne hadn't noticed Meg having more than a routine relationship with any man, either among the gang members who invaded Verdant Valley or at the encampment. No one except her father. Marne thought about Meg's advice on how to deal with Clint when she first arrived at the Spawn encampment. Was there more to the father and daughter than she'd realized?

Meg nodded but didn't speak of her ambitions or her secrets.

"Each configuration of the cowries has a proverb associated with it," Jumoke said. "The proverb for this one is 'A king is made by his own hand.' Yemaya promises that with her help you can achieve what you most desire. You don't have to tell me what that is. Yemaya knows."

At first, Meg maintained her stoic expressing, unwilling or unable to share her thoughts. "Duke has not been a good leader for us," she said.

"Can you and, ah, Yemaya," she waved toward the altar to her left, "give someone the magic they need to overthrow him?"

"Do you want to bring down your leader?" Jumoke's voice was almost a whisper.

Marne realized that as often happened with divination, something that started as educational had become something much more.

Meg looked around as though afraid someone might be listening and then nodded.

"We were strong and prosperous under Junior," Meg said, her words slow and deliberate, "but now we're filled with an inner rot that is destroying the gang. Duke is sacrificing some of us to enrich the rest." She shook her head. "He won't stop until he has destroyed everything. Everyone's afraid of him and his people. Clint sees to it."

She looked at Marne. "That one wasn't intimidated by Clint or Duke. How was that possible? She's just a girl. She had nothing."

"And what do you want?" Jumoke said, bringing the conversation back to Meg. "Clint's your father. You're not afraid of him, are you? Aren't there others who would stand with you?"

What about the father of your child? Marne thought but didn't say. Won't he stand with you?

"If you can really deny Duke's demands," Meg said, "he'll make Clint punish those who stood against him—even if it destroys the gang. We can't stand up to him and survive."

The conversation sparked by the divination continued for some time. Meg talked about how power was won and lost within the gang. What happened when Junior disappeared. How Duke gained control and what it would take to wrest that control away from him.

Jumoke questioned Meg, challenging her assumptions that those with less power could not overthrow those dominating them. Even though she had an introduction to the idea, Marne noticed it was hard for Meg to see a third way for dealing with the tyranny of Duke. The proverb Jumoke quoted at the beginning of their session described the flow of power within the Demon Spawn. There was no natural chain of command. When one leader became weak, his position was thrown open to whoever had the strength to seize it. If someone could defeat Duke and convince the gang to follow him, that one would become the new leader.

"As I understand what you're saying," Jumoke said at last, "when we repulse Duke and his followers, there may be a power vacuum."

Meg nodded.

"Then you can be the link. Between the old regime and what is to come," Jumoke said. "Between your people and the people here. Between the women of your gang and the Sisterhood."

After a moment, Meg nodded again.

"As I see it," Jumoke continued, "you can be what we call the kingmaker. The one who will identify and install your new leader."

Meg stared at Jumoke, then smiled as though realizing the power she would hold.

Jumoke pushed her advantage. "Have you thought of who that person should be?"

Meg shook her head.

"What qualities would he need?" Jumoke asked.

Meg considered, and then said, "He would need to be strong enough to stand up to Duke. To defeat him. He would have to be someone people will follow. If this plays out as you're planning, he would have the support of the women we recruit. And maybe a connection back to your people, at least for a while."

Jumoke stood up and walked to her altar. After bowing toward the pot that was the home to Yemaya, she reached behind it. When she sat back down at the table, she said, "This isn't how a divination session is usually conducted. But I believe Yemaya brought you to us for a reason. All the Orisha have power, but she is their queen. She has the power to give you what you want."

Marne wondered where Jumoke was going, as this certainly wasn't normal. Her godmother placed a necklace in the middle of the cowries spread out on the table. A piece of Yemaya's sacred stone, the deep sky-blue turquoise from the southern reaches of the Republic, hung from the chain.

Meg's eyes widened. She recognized the rare gemstone for what it was.

"You think this turquoise is valuable because there are few like it in the world," Jumoke said. "But its value lies in its connection to Yemaya, the Great Mother, the owner of all *ashé*, all power. Through it you can tell her what it is you want. Whisper your aspirations to this stone and Yemaya will hear it, wherever you are. When you find the one you want to rule your people, give that person this turquoise and you will make a new king."

Meg and Marne stared at the necklace. Marne had never heard of turquoise having sacred powers, but she felt the magic of Jumoke's words. She thought Meg could feel it as well.

"Give me your hands," Jumoke commanded.

Meg held her hands over the table. Jumoke turned them palm up so they were in the shape of giving and receiving. Then she picked up the necklace. "This stone contains powerful magic. Whoever possesses it can make himself king." She placed it in Meg's hands and wrapped them around it.

Before closing this most unusual session, Jumoke told Meg that whoever owned the turquoise also had an obligation to Yemaya.

"When you go home, you must take seven rocks and pile them in a pyramid by the front door of your house. Each morning you must refresh them with cool water and thank Yemaya for all she has given you. Do you understand?"

Meg opened her hands and looked wide-eyed from the necklace to Jumoke's face. Then she nodded.

Marne wondered whether Meg would recognize the two small shrines she had left in front of Master Clint's trailer. What would she do with them?

"When you give the turquoise to your new king, he must put seven rocks in front of his home. If he no longer wants this stone, he must throw it away in running water. Otherwise, its magic will turn against him." Jumoke stared at Meg until she looked away.

"Look at me," Jumoke commanded.

Meg looked back at her.

"I've given you great power," Jumoke said.

"Thank you," Meg whispered, slipping the necklace over her head and tucking it beneath her shirt.

CHAPTER 16

"We have thirteen visiting Demon Spawn women and their children," Lola told Marne as the two of them prepared for yet another council meeting. "They are tucked away in compounds around the village, but I don't think we will be able to hide them much longer."

Their plan was working better than expected. Every day families of the Spawn arrived at Marne's granny's workshop, often two or three. Never together but as a constant stream. The women of the Sisterhood found places for them in the compounds of their husbands and fathers. Never more than a single mother and her children in any one compound. So far their Demon Spawn visitors remained invisible. But soon there would be too many of them to hide.

"Duke and his people will be looking for their tribute soon," Lola continued. "It's time to share our plan with Malik and the Hunters Guild. They shouldn't be surprised. We know Meg told Clint so I'm sure Malik, Akande and Hackett had a good laugh about it, too."

Marne knew when Meg told Master Clint of their scheme he thought it was a great joke. According to Meg he couldn't imagine that the women of Verdant Valley posed any threat to his plans. Master Duke derided them as market women and artisans — weaklings who would have to submit to his demands. It was as though Clint forgot the way Marne gained control over him.

Soon Marne and Lola were at another tedious council meeting where nothing of substance could be done under the baleful eye of Master Clint and the other Demon Spawn. Another meeting where Akande watched Marne while pulling his lower lip between his teeth with slow, sensual strokes, as though promising her some future delights. Another meeting where Master Clint stared at her, his eyes reminding her what she had given to him and then taken away. All she could think about was how much she wanted to escape them both.

When the meeting ended, Marne saw Lola pull Malik and Akande into a whispered conference. When Master Clint joined them, Marne wondered how Lola would separate the *obanla* and his deputy from their Demon Spawn shadows for a visit to the Hunters Guild.

After a moment, Meg joined the conversation. Marne watched as she pulled her father away and down the hall.

After Meg and Master Clint left, Lola motioned to Marne and soon they were following Malik and Akande out the front gate of the *obanla's* compound. As they made their way through the village square, Marne frowned remembering when she and Akande made this same trip, and their detour. She was glad they were with Malik and Lola this time.

Caught up in her thoughts, she fell a few steps behind the others. Akande slowed and, behind Lola's back, grabbed Marne's hand. "Come along, Little Bird," he murmured. Marne tried to pull away, but he wouldn't release her. The rest of the way to the Guild Hall, he alternately ran his thumb up and down the side of her hand and squeezed it. She stared straight ahead, pretending he didn't exist.

Once the Hunters Guild was assembled, Malik invited Marne to tell them about the battle preparations she witnessed at the Demon Spawn encampment.

"How many gang members do you think there were?" Hackett, the head of the Guild, asked her.

She looked at the people surrounding her.

"As many as you…" She waved her hand toward them. They smiled. "… on each side of the battle. Plus more wrestling and fighting." She finished. Their eyes widened. It was a sizable force before they considered that all the Demon Spawn had firearms while, the Guild had not been very successful acquiring their own munitions.

"Thank you, Marne," Malik said before anyone could question her further. Akande patted the seat next to him, but Marne chose a chair next to Lola instead. She wanted to stay as far from him as possible.

Malik turned back to the Guild members. "As we've talked about before, as members of the council," he nodded toward Lola, "we think these are overwhelming odds." He let the Guild digest this information.

"Lola tells me that there is a group of women who have been trying to find a different solution," Malik said. "One that doesn't require that we take up arms against the Demon Spawn." He motioned Lola to the front of the room.

Lola stood for a long time surveying her audience. Marne wondered whether she too was imagining the carnage that would result from the Guild's plan to resist the gang.

"I don't need to remind you what is at stake here," Lola began. "If we bow to them, there will be famine throughout Verdant Valley and the entire Reserve. I've talked to Talé and the other farm managers. Not only can we not survive through the winter, there won't be enough seed remaining for next spring's planting." She paused, looking from face to face. "And we suspect the Spawn is already planning on an even more oppressive tribute next year. I know the Guild means well, but there is no way you can vanquish the Spawn. Even if you had superior firepower, which you don't, and even if you had Rangers trained by the Republic instead of farmers and guards, which you don't, the Spawn's superior numbers will defeat you."

Marne could see the faces around her harden as the Guild drew themselves up in their chairs as though preparing to argue their case against Lola's facts.

"She's right," someone called out. "We can't defeat the Spawn. We've been playing at being fighters, but they are the masters."

Heads nodded around the room. Marne was surprised the hunters conceded so easily. But then, they knew what they were up against. They must have always known their plan was hopeless.

" Some of us from the Market Board," Lola continued, "have spent most of the last month trying to find another way of dealing with the Demon Spawn. A way that saves Verdant Valley and the Reserve without massacring our own people."

Several members of the Guild leaned forward. Marne thought maybe they, too, had been looking for a third way, another solution to the problem of the Demon Spawn and their tribute demands.

Lola described the Sisterhood of the Moon and Marne's discovery of what happened to their first tribute. She depicted the condition of the women and children Marne had seen at the encampment.

"We would never allow members of our village to have more than they need while others were making their children go hungry," Lola said. "Even before this challenge, the council was working on plans to ensure that everyone in our village and everyone in the Reserve would have enough to survive the coming winter."

As the local police force, Guild members were often the first to discover people and compounds who through bad luck or mismanagement were no longer maintaining themselves. It was the Guild, working with the *obanla* and his staff, that ensured those who needed help got it.

Then Lola told the group the Sisterhood's plan of providing for those Demon Spawn whom their leaders had abandoned.

"Spawn women and their children have been arriving in Verdant Valley for over a week now," she explained. "And we expect more in the run-up to the tribute deadline. This has been a covert operation so far—

although some of you must have noticed *oyimbo* 'visitors' in your compounds."

Marne looked around. Some people looked surprised, but others were nodding as though grasping a mystery that had eluded them.

"We won't be able to keep our activities a secret much longer," Lola explained. "There will be too many of them to ignore. Now, we are ready to take the next step of our plan. For that we need the support of both the Guild and the Council."

That evening, Marne and Anana settled into the easy chairs of Marne's sitting room. Now that the sun set earlier, it was often too cool to meet in the plaza, so they had moved their after-work get-togethers inside. As had become her habit, Kandy Lynn and her children joined them. The children played with Kara at the women's feet. As Anana had hoped, Kandy Lynn's children, a boy about her son's age and a girl a couple of years older, had become great friends.

The women, too, were becoming friends. Kandy Lynn still insisted on referring to Marne as Clint's "old lady," giving her some measure of unearned respect with the despicable title. While Marne and Anana talked about the workings of the Council, Kandy Lynn spoke about the way the gang worked.

"There are lots of gangs like ours," Kandy Lynn explained to them. "People who couldn't live under the boot heel of the Republic. We live in encampments, like the one you visited," Kandy Lynn nodded toward Marne. "Each gang has their own territory. We'd rather fight the Rangers, the Republic law enforcement pigs, than our fellow gang members."

She never explained how the Demon Spawn and the other gangs survived out in the vast deserts of the Republic. Marne surmised they were all bandits, raiding the small towns and settlements and taking what they wanted.

"You're not the only people paying us tribute," Kandy Lynn said. "But you're the only people with food. There's drought everywhere. As Duke said when he took over from my old man, you need to take from those who have."

Marne wondered how long Verdant Valley had been paying a tribute to the Demon Spawn. She had never heard about it until this season.

Tonight while they were talking, the sound of a solitary motorcycle pushed its way into the compound courtyard. The three women looked at one another.

"Stay here," Marne commanded as she jumped to her feet and ran to the front door. Before she opened it, she stopped and took a deep breath. She hadn't had a confrontation with Master Clint since her return from the encampment, but now that respite had come to an end.

"Where is she?" Master Clint stood in the middle of the courtyard. His face was invisible behind the darkened faceplate of his helmet, but his angry voice was unmistakable. "Where is that wench?"

Pulling herself up tall, Marne joined the knot of people who gawked at Master Clint as he raged on. Although he continued to wear his gun, Master Clint had quit wearing his jacket and leggings around the *obanla's* compound. Apparently he felt his mere presence was intimidating enough. But now he was decked out, black leather chaps and jacket, bandoliers crisscrossing his chest, topped off by the helmet with the snake-like demon embossed on the side. He personified the entire gang.

After a long moment of silence, Marne's grandfather, their *oba*, stepped forward. Master Clint took off his helmet and glared at him.

"Welcome to our humble compound," her grandfather said. His authority as the compound head was unmistakable. "Who are you looking for?"

Ignoring the greeting, Master Clint looked through the crowd. Marne saw his eyes find her, then skip to someone behind her. She turned to see Kandy Lynn had followed her out of the apartment. Marne reached back, grabbed the woman's hand, and pulled her forward. There wasn't much the two of them could do against Master Clint but at least they would stand together.

The crowd parted as the two women stepped forward to stand next to the *oba*.

"What are you doing here?" Master Clint growled.

The *oba* looked from the women to Master Clint. Granny, as the most senior woman of the family, had talked to her husband about the Demon Spawn living in his compound, both Meg and Kandy Lynn. He wasn't happy with the idea but he hadn't forbidden it.

"I-I..." Kandy Lynn began.

"She is my guest, our guest," Marne said, glaring back at Master Clint. This was the first test of the Sisterhood's plan. If the compounds didn't protect their *oyimbo* visitors, the plan would disintegrate.

"You don't belong here," Master Clint said to Kandy Lynn, ignoring both Marne and her grandfather. "Get your things and scurry back to the encampment, before Duke notices you're missing."

Kandy Lynn tightened her hold on Marne's hand.

"No," she said, her voice stronger. "I'm a free woman. I go where I please."

Her response surprised Marne. At the encampment Kandy Lynn had appeared to beaten down. Marne hadn't expected her to accept her invitation to Verdant Valley, let alone stand up to Master Clint.

"Don't challenge me, woman," Master Clint swung his leg off the cycle and stood beside it.

Marne felt rather than saw the compound guards, led by the *baala*, her grandfather's deputy, step forward.

"The woman is our guest," the *baala* said. "She is free to stay or go as she wills."

Marne watched Kandy Lynn and Master Clint stare at each other. After a tense moment, Master Clint broke his eye contact with Kandy Lynn to look at Marne. Then he moved his glance to the *oba*.

"She shouldn't be here," Master Clint said, and then moved his glance from the *oba* back to Kandy Lynn. "Don't push Duke too hard," he said to her. "These people can't protect you if you continue to defy him."

"These people," Kandy Lynn waved her arm around the compound, "have done more for me and mine than Duke ever did. And you can tell him so." She dropped Marne's hand, turned, and walked away.

"Duke won't have you if you defy him and you know you can't make it as a lone wolf," Master Clint yelled at Kandy Lynn's back. She slipped into the apartment without any response.

Master Clint returned his gaze to Marne. "What about you, darlin'," he said, his tone softer. "When're you comin' back to me?"

Without a word, Marne turned and followed Kandy Lynn to the apartment. Would she ever be free from Master Clint's lechery?

The next evening, Lola, Marne, and Anana strolled toward Marne's granny's little house for another meeting of the Sisterhood. It was a bit of a walk from their compound, but Lola insisted both she and the girls needed the exercise. As they walked, Marne wondered what happened at the other compounds. Had those *obas* given their women the kind of tongue-lashing her grandfather had given her and Anana? He had upbraided them for bringing the compound under the scrutiny of what he called "our Demon Spawn masters." She was proud of her father and Anana's mother- and father-in-law. They stood up for the girls and their commitment to finding a third way out of this battle with the Demon Spawn. Both families felt they couldn't withdraw from the commitments they had made to her granny and Jumoke. Granny's word held much weight among her sons and grandsons. Partway through his scolding, Marne realized that her grandfather, too, deferred to the power of the mother of his children.

Tonight, her granny had asked Marne, Anana, and Lola to come a little early to help her set up and get ready. Although Granny told them her arm was healing, it was still in the sling that prevented her from doing more than supervise their efforts. Lola and Anana went into the sitting room to arrange the chairs and central altar. Marne joined Gladys in the cooking room to put together the drinks and nibbles.

Soon Granny was at the door, welcoming the rest of the women. Marne distributed mugs, pots of hot tea, and platters while the women settled themselves. Again there were the deep-indigo bowl inscribed with a crescent moon, a candle, and a bowl of water on the table in the center of the circle.

"Where is Meg?" Talé asked when everyone else arrived. She looked at Lola. "Didn't she come with you?"

"I haven't seen her all day," Lola said, frowning. "I wonder if she went back to the encampment."

"No," Anana said. "She and Master Clint have been in and out of Malik's private sitting room all day." She smiled. "I don't know what all they talked about, but I do know Master Clint was livid about all the gang members who have migrated into Verdant Valley."

"Perhaps we should wait a few minutes," Talé suggested. "I'm sure Meg will make it if she can."

"In the meantime," Jumoke said looking around, "why don't you each tell how it is going with our guests. Is everyone settling in?"

The women erupted, each telling the story of their visitors and their own visit from Master Clint or one of the other gang members.

"Wait, wait," Jumoke said, holding up her hand. "One at a time." She looked at Marne. "I heard Master Clint himself visited your compound."

Marne nodded. "I don't understand the relationships among the Spawn. I don't think they marry as we do. But the father of Kandy Lynn's children used to be the leader of the gang, before Master Duke. She's alone now. I think Master Clint threatened to throw her and her children out of the gang."

"The encounter upset her," Anana said, shaking her head. "But she didn't leave. At least not yet."

When Marne and Anana finished, Jumoke spoke up. She told about a similar encounter between one of the Demon Spawn and the woman she was sheltering. Then, going around the circle, the other women told similar stories. Stories of intimidation by the Spawn and courage on the part of their guests and the leading men of their compounds.

After telling her own story, Talé turned to Lola. "You have the ear of the Market Board. What have your members told you?"

"The same thing. At first, no one wanted to have anything to do with those women and children. Not until they saw how hungry they were, especially the children." She took a deep breath. "So far, everyone's determined to see this through."

The women nodded, each remembering her own experiences of confronting the Demon Spawn. In the silence that filled the room, Marne heard a motorcycle come down the road and stop.

Granny stood up. "There she is now," she said, standing up to greet Meg. Before she could get to the door, it slammed open.

"You all have to leave," Meg shouted. "He can't find you here."

CHAPTER 17

Gladys led Meg into the sitting room while Jumoke jumped up and grabbed the bowl of water from the altar. She shut the door, saying the prayer to Eleggua, the keeper of entrances and exits. "*Ashé*," she said loud enough for everyone to hear.

"*Ashé*, so be it," they responded. Prayer wouldn't keep out an angry Master Clint, but Marne knew the women felt better when the doorway had been ritually sealed.

In the meantime, Talé and Lola, who were sitting on either side of the chair they'd left empty for Meg, encouraged her to sit down. Today she had resumed wearing what Marne thought of as her complete costume: black leather jacket and pants, black gloves, black boots. She set her helmet with its awful image of a snake-like demon on the floor next to her. Lola handed her a mug of hot tea.

Jumoke returned to the sitting room, replaced the bowl on the table, and lit the candle.

After a moment of silence, she nodded toward Lola who was their leader.

"We were waiting for you to arrive," Lola said.

Meg held the mug in her hands but hadn't taken a sip. Marne saw she was agitated and impatient with the slowness of the women to respond to her.

"Now," Lola continued, "tell us what's going on."

Meg took a deep breath. "Clint is coming right behind me. I told him about your group and your plans." She looked around the circle. "You said I should."

The women nodded, agreeing and encouraging her to continue.

"He's so angry with you, with everyone." She paused as if catching her breath. "I don't want any of you to get hurt. If you leave right now, you can escape." She looked into the steaming liquid. "Otherwise... I don't know, I don't know what he'll do."

The room was silent as they waited for the thunder of another cycle. Marne saw fear on the women's faces.

"We should stay," Talé said, her voice low and calm. "If we're not here, he'll track each of us down. We're stronger together."

Jumoke nodded. "I agree. We don't want to take his anger back to our compounds."

After a long pause, the other women nodded. They had already faced down the Demon Spawn in the compounds. They would stand against Master Clint together.

Lola turned back to Meg. "Thank you," she said, patting the woman's leg. "You did exactly as we asked. Now we must face the consequences."

Lola looked around the room as if gauging the level of their fear. "We are meeting tonight to discuss the next step in our plan. I suggest we go ahead with that while we wait for Master Clint. We'll deal with him when he arrives."

Looking at Meg, she continued, "Before you arrived, we recounted our experiences with your people. Your women and their children are enjoying their visits to our compounds. The *obas* who are our family heads are standing strong against Spawn efforts to remove them." She paused. "Isn't that what we said?"

The other women nodded.

"Now, it's time for your women and our women to learn more about each other so they can work together. What would be the best way to do that?"

Silence enveloped the room. Feeding the Demon Spawn women wasn't enough. The Sisterhood had to prevent Master Clint and his men from destroying Verdant Valley when they discovered there would be no more tribute.

"A party," Anana said. "We should have a party for our guests. Marne and I have been talking to Kandy Lynn. We've also shared some of our plans for a third-way response to the Demon Spawn's demands. Perhaps we could use a get-together to talk to everyone at once."

Silence followed, then heads nodded in agreement.

"A party," Lola said. "How would we do that?"

"We can't use the space below the *obanla's* compound without telling Malik, the Council, and their watchers what we're planning," Talé said, thinking out loud.

"The Market Board has a large meeting room," Marne's granny said. She turned to Lola. "Could we use that?"

Lola appeared to still be considering Anana's suggestion. Then she smiled. "The Market Board hall. The board can invite all the women for a… hmm, what shall we call it?"

"An end-of-the-market season celebration," Granny said. "We've never done that before, everyone's too tired, but we could this year."

"Yes," Lola nodded, "Our first, ah, Annual Harvest Festival for all the women of the village, and their guests. Perfect." She paused. "We can update everyone about our plans and talk to our guests about the next steps."

Suddenly, everyone was talking at once, making suggestions and offering ideas. Soon they had a plan.

Finally, Lola said, "That's it. Everyone has their assignments. In three days, at the Market Board hall."

"That's only two days before the Demon Spawn expect their tribute," Jumoke reminded them. "Is that enough time?"

Lola thought for a long moment, then nodded. "It will take all the other members of the Board and all of our guests, but we can be ready."

After not saying anything since her arrival, Meg exploded. "Are you people crazy? You're planning on fighting Duke, Clint, and the others with a party?" Her voice rose. "A party?"

The women were silent, then Lola said, "Yes, dear. That's exactly what we're going to do," she smiled. "It will be fun."

All the women were smiling and laughing as though they shared a secret joke.

Lola patted Meg's leg again. "You and I need to talk. You will have a special part to play. But when you tell Master Clint about this meeting, and you will, I don't want you to know all the details."

In the silence that followed, Marne heard a motorcycle approaching.

"Now, you all need to leave," Granny said, cocking her head as though listening.

"No." Lola's voice was sharp. "We're not leaving you alone to face what's coming." She held out her mug. "Marne, dear," she said. "I need more tea, if you could. Jumoke, could you close out our ritual?

Marne refilled the women's mugs and then went to the cooking room for more tea from the large pot she was keeping warm on the stove.

In the meantime, Jumoke stood up, blew out the candle, picked up the bowl, and tossed the water onto the front porch. Marne heard her quiet "*Modupue*, thank you."

When Marne returned, the women had moved the small altar to the back of the room and added another chair to the circle.

"You people are crazy," Meg muttered as they listened to the approaching cycle.

"No," Lola said, "We're just a bunch of, what did he call us? Oh, yes, we're just a bunch of artisans and market women enjoying tea together. Nothing to be afraid of."

"Pinkun! Pinkun! Ajanbiti! We are *Iyami,* we are the mothers." The women chanted as they waited.

Marne was still laughing to herself the next morning. As expected, Meg had watched gap-mouthed as the Sisterhood invited Master Clint into their gathering, insisting he join them for tea and nibbles.

Before he could say anything, Jumoke turned to Marne's granny and said, "Now, what about your young Nathan and my Alice. They'd make a lovely pair and their children, oh, their children." She rolled her eyes in apparent ecstasy.

"She's young yet," Granny responded. "Do you think she's ready?" She looked at the other women.

Like a gaggle of geese all the women responded at once. Soon everyone was offering an opinion about the proposed union, and the children that might result. Everyone except Marne, Anana, and, of course, Meg. While the older women talked, Marne looked at Anana, raising her eyebrow as if to ask, Who are these women talking about? There was no Alice in their compound and the only Nathan Marne knew was still in diapers.

Marne watched as the women blathered on and on about other imaginary people, proposing unions or strategizing ways to separate non-existent young lovers. They discussed wedding planning and appropriated bride prices. Whenever Master Clint tried to interrupt, they spoke louder, ignoring him. When it appeared they had exhausted all of the imaginary young couples of Verdant Valley, several of the women slipped into memories of the men they had known. They discussed the ones they married and the ones who got away. Marne recognized some of those men's names. She wondered whether the women had moved from fantasy to reality. Finally, there was a pause, as everyone seemed to take a breath at the same time.

"How about you, Meg," Granny asked, turning toward their Demon Spawn sister. "Marne seems to think there is no one in your life, but that can't be so, a handsome young woman like you. Surely your father has found someone for you. Or has he set your price too high?"

They all looked at Meg, who shook her head. Marne wasn't sure whether she was denying a hidden lover or her own desirability. When her hand slipped to her belly as it had during the divination session with Jumoke, Marne knew there had to be someone back at the encampment. Someone who had remained hidden during Marne's short time there. What did Master Clint think about her condition? Did he even know?

"You haven't neglected your daughter, have you, Master Clint?" Granny asked, turning toward him. "Why doesn't your daughter have her own children to look after?"

Marne could see that Master Clint was startled by this turn in the conversation. For a moment it looked like he forgot he was the enforcer who had come out to her granny's home to stop their meeting. Instead, his face took on that disconcerted look men often assumed when confronted by older women prying into their personal affairs.

"I-ah-I," he stuttered, his cheeks reddening.

Before he could recover, all of the older women gave him advice about what he should do, the sort of man who would make a good mate for his daughter, and how to determine an appropriate price for her. Now Marne watched red shame creep up Meg's neck as their suggestions became increasingly explicit.

Finally, Granny held up her hand. "Stop," she told the other women. "It isn't appropriate to talk about this in the girl's presence. You're embarrassing her."

Meg's blush only deepened as the women's laughter filled the sitting room.

"It's late," Jumoke said as the laugher died away. "This old lady is tired," she stood up. "Thank you, Gladys, for a lovely evening. Master Clint, Meg, you must visit with us again."

Without waiting for a reply she gathered up her things and sashayed out of the room and away from the house. As if on cue, all the other women also stood, thanked Granny, and made their way outside. Soon only Marne and her granny, Meg and her father remained.

Meg glared at them. Her blush had faded, replaced by livid rage. Without a word, she grabbed her helmet and marched out the door. A moment later, they heard the roar of her cycle.

Clint glanced from Marne to her granny. He looked dazed. Before he could recover, Marne stood, took the mug from his hand, gathered up several other mugs, and headed for the cooking room. She wanted to get away before he realized what they had done to him.

Modupue, thank you, Eleggua, she thought. You have saved us. At least for tonight.

"Did you come all the way out here for a reason?" Marne heard her granny ask.

Without responding, she heard Master Clint stand up. As he opened the outside door, he stopped. "Don't you ever do that to me again," he snarled. In a moment, they heard a second cycle making its way toward the main road.

As Marne walked back into the sitting room to finish cleaning up, her granny burst into another round of laughter. "Your Master Clint isn't so strong after all," she said, tears running down her cheeks.

Marne smiled as she picked up the rest of the debris from the meeting. "No," she conceded. "He isn't."

That was last night. As Marne made her way over to the Market Board guildhall Guild Hall this morning, she wondered what havoc Master Clint would bring down upon the members of the Sisterhood. How would he punish them for the way they had treated him? She had wanted to apologize to Meg, but she hadn't been in the apartment when Marne had made it home. She wondered whether they had lost their seventh sister in trying to protect themselves from Master Clint. Only time would tell.

CHAPTER 18

When Marne and Anana arrived at the Market Hall the next morning Lola and Talé were already there, converting the meeting space into a party room with an open area at one end for socializing and tables and chairs at the other end for the luncheon. The tables were covered with yellow and brown cloths in the spirit of the harvest season. There was a pumpkin on each table in honor of Oshun, an eggplant for Oya, and small toys for Eleggua and the children.

Marne drifted toward the extravagant altar display Lola and Talé had built against one of the walls. The space was draped with brown and gold cloths similar to those on the tables. As was appropriate for a Market Board event, the centerpiece was the Orisha Oya, their patron. The women had brought the giant ceramic pot that held Oya's tools and presence from its regular home in one of the back rooms of the hall and placed it on a five-foot-tall pedestal. Ribbons of every color swirled behind the container in a tornado of excitement. Change was in the air. Containers for the other Orisha surrounded Oya's pot. The metal pot of Ogun, the warrior Orisha and patron of the Hunters Guild, sat on the floor directly below Oya as though protecting her. And of course, next to Ogun was the effigy of Eleggua, the trickster who guarded their doorways and taught them to watch for the unexpected opening. The whole area was surrounded by a knee-high picket fence to keep the *oyimbo* women and their children out of the sacred space.

Everything the Sisterhood needed was represented on that altar, if they wanted to play out the drama Lola, Talé, and Gladys were constructing. Working together the women of Verdant Valley and the Demon Spawn women could protect themselves and their children.

"*Ashé,*" Marne whispered. "May it be so."

With that prayer, she walked across the room to help Talé put the final decorations on the long serving table set near the far wall. Tomorrow was the next step in the Sisterhood's plan. Marne knew Talé would explain how there was enough for everyone but only if everyone shared. The people of Verdant Valley did not want their Demon Spawn guests and their children to starve but they needed to be able feed their own families, too. The Demon Spawn women knew that their leaders were stealing from them and their children. The women of Verdant Valley needed to convince them to stand together in defiance of their leaders. All the women needed to realize that if Master Duke took everything to sell for more weapons, then everyone would starve.

Lola had used the story of the Golden Goose to explain the problem to the sisters. In that story a farmer had a goose that laid a golden egg every day. Eventually the farmer got greedy and killed the goose thinking that there was a collection of golden eggs in its body. Of course, he was mistaken. Not only were there no golden eggs, the goose was dead and there would be no more golden eggs.

The people of Verdant Valley were like the goose that provided a golden egg every year to the Demon Spawn. However, if Master Duke destroyed them, there would be no more golden eggs, no more tributes.

Even though she had been part of the planning, Marne wondered how Lola and Talé would convince the Demon Spawn women to challenge Master Clint and his warriors. What could the Sisterhood, artisans and market women, do to persuade them to join in their third way? How could they thwart both the Demon Spawn and their own Hunters Guild members?

For the festival luncheon Lola had asked all the Verdant Valley women to bring a small dish to share, nothing extravagant, just enough for themselves, their children, and their guests. As she had explained at their meeting, the goal was to show the Demon Spawn women that there was enough for everyone as long as no one got greedy. At the end of the meal, the Sisterhood wanted everyone to be satisfied without excessive amounts of food left over.

Marne looked around the room. The Sisterhood had very carefully set the stage. All that was required was for everyone, including their nemesis, Master Duke, to play their part.

The next afternoon, as Marne and the other young women began to clear away the debris from the Sisterhood's luncheon, Lola and Talé stood up. Gradually, the conversations around the room quieted.

"Thank you all for joining us for this First Annual Harvest Festival. I want to recognize all our guests, especially Li'l Meg and Kandy Lynn who have worked so hard to ensure that their sisters and their children have found accommodations among our compounds."

Polite applause followed as the women smiled at their Demon Spawn guests, many of whom were wrapping the food remaining on their plates into cloths. Marne knew even though the compounds were taking care of the women and their children, future scarcity was always in the back of the women's minds.

Lola smiled at the women and their children. "We women of Verdant Valley have some things to say to our guests, but first Anana and a couple of her friends have set up a play area in the back of the room. All of the children are invited to join them while we women talk."

At first nothing happened. Then, several of the Verdant Valley children ran over to the play area. When Kandy Lynn led her children to Anana, several of the other Spawn women followed. Soon, the children had been sorted by age and were playing together.

When all the women returned to their seats, Lola continued. "It was only six days ago when Kandy Lynn first brought her children here to visit Marne and her family. The rest of you followed. I know most of you know the story, but I've asked her to tell us why she came and what's happened since she's been here." She nodded to Kandy Lynn, who was sitting at Lola's table.

"I'm not going to tell you all what my life has been like since Junior disappeared. It's been hard for all of us. Then I met Clint's hag—well, she says she's not Clint's hag, but..." she let the idea hang in the air. "Marne invited me here. She said her people would feed my babies." She paused. "And they did." A look of astonishment filled her face as though she was still surprised. "My children are not crying themselves to sleep anymore." She turned toward the play area. "Look at them. Look at all of them. Coming here is the best thing I've ever done."

Silence filled the room as she returned to her chair.

"Me, too," someone shouted.

"Me, too," another voice said.

Then the room was filled with shouting women.

Lola held up her hands and slowly the women quieted.

"We welcomed Kandy Lynn and the rest of you as our sisters," she said. "But we have a problem." She let her words fill the silence. She nodded toward Talé.

"My family owns High Valley Fields, the largest farm in Babapupa." Talé walked over to stand in front of the long serving tables with their now empty containers. Unlike the other Verdant Valley women who were dressed in traditional wrappers and head ties, she was wearing her farm uniform of work pants and a long-sleeved tee with the High Valley logo. "Last year, after paying our tribute to you, we sold about eighty percent of the remainder of our harvest to Scarlet Dawn and the other villages of the Reserve. We kept the rest to feed ourselves and our children and as seed for the following year."

While she talked, workers from the farm pushed the tables apart, piling about a quarter of the empty bowls on one table and adding a sign "Demon Spawn Tribute." They put another sign "Babapupa Reserve" in the center of the remaining table with two small piles at one end with "Verdant Valley" on one sign and "Seeds" on the other. Finally they pulled up an empty table. They put a "Republic of the Southwest" sign in the middle of it.

"Years ago we were able to sell some of our harvest to the Republic, but with the drought that is no longer possible. The drought's been hard on everyone. This year our harvest is down. As far as we can tell, there are also food shortages throughout the Republic. So even if we had money, there is nothing to buy. Now we're living year-to-year, hoping the rains come."

She paused, allowing the women to grasp the situation.

"Even though our harvest was down this year, the Council decided to maintain our tribute to the Spawn." One of Talé's people stood in front of the Demon Spawn table to prevent the workers from taking any containers from it. "Because we've agreed to give away a larger part of our harvest, some of us and our brothers and sisters throughout the Reserve will go hungry. We won't starve but none of us will be getting fat."

Talé looked over the crowd. Marne pulled her eyes away from the drama at the serving tables to gauge the women's reaction. Even though the Verdant Valley women knew the basic story, it was obvious that many of them didn't realize how desperate their situation was becoming. She had a harder time assessing the Spawn women's reaction. Some were wide-eyed with surprise, but most sat stony-faced as though unwilling to accept Talé's words.

Then the farm workers began removing the containers from the Demon Spawn table. "Now, we've discovered that your leaders aren't using our tribute to feed you and your children. Instead, they are selling our tribute to buy weapons. Now they want more from us." When the Demon Spawn table was empty, Talé's workers joined hands around the Babapupa and "Seed" tables, as though protecting them.

"Master Duke is training your young men to force us to give you an additional tribute. And, as I'm sure you all know, our leaders are training members of our Hunters Guild to defend our remaining stores. Tomorrow when your forces come, our people intend to fight back. People will die, your husbands, fathers, and sons. Our husbands, fathers, and sons, too. And then more people will die. If our forces are successful, you will not be able to feed yourselves and your children. If your forces are successful, we will not be able to feed our children and ourselves. If you take all of our harvest, there will be nothing to plant in the spring. Next year there will be no tribute at all."

The only sounds in the room were from the children playing.

"Will Master Clint use this second tribute to feed you and your children or will we starve to buy more guns for your warriors?"

As if on cue, the front door of the hall slammed open. Before anyone could react, Clint and Duke, with some of their men, stomped into the room. As they had the first time they invaded the council meeting, again they wore their black leather jackets and bandoliers full of bullets. Guns hung from their hips.

Talé stepped back but Lola was on her feet and moving through the tables toward the men.

"Master Duke, Master Clint. Welcome." She smiled at the two leaders. "Welcome to our Harvest Festival. You're too late for lunch." She nodded toward the decimated serving tables, their signs suddenly absent. "But please join me for some coffee and conversation." Without giving the Demon Spawn a chance to respond, she waved at the workers who stood by the serving table and turned to lead the two men toward the front of the room. "We were just discussing our mutual situation, perhaps you can enlighten us …"

"Stop." Master Clint's voice boomed through the room, drawing all eyes toward him. Even the children playing in the corner were silent.

"We did not give you permission for a secret meeting." Master Duke looked from one table to another, scowling at the women. "You people are not allowed to…"

"This is hardly a secret meeting," Lola interrupted him. "We have many of your own women and children here. And I'm sure Master Clint's daughter told you all about what we are doing." She smiled at Li'l Meg, who had come to stand beside her.

"Out. Out." Master Clint shouted, waving toward the door.

No one moved. Then Lola smiled and gestured to one side and then to the other. "Thank you all for helping us celebrate this year's harvest, especially our Demon Spawn guests. Remember, there is enough for everyone if we share. May this be the beginning of a long and fruitful relationship between us."

Suddenly the room was full of sound and movement. Women retrieving their children from the play area. Women searching through the debris around the serving table for their containers. Women chattering as they made their way out of the hall. The women swirled around Lola, Meg, the two Demon Spawn men who stood at the center of the room glowering at everyone, and the others who stood on either side of the door.

Marne's granny and Jumoke stood by the exit smiling at the women leaving, hugging them, and whispering in their ears. As planned, Anana and Marne were outside the hall. They handed each of the Demon Spawn women a small, gold-painted wooden egg. Marne noticed that Anana patted her son Karamat's head as Kandy Lynn carried him along with her own children from the hall. Marne hoped the Demon Spawn woman would be able to keep the children safe during what was to follow.

As the women were leaving, Talé and her workers began cleaning up the remains of the party. When all their guests were gone, Lola was left standing in the center of the room flanked by the other members of the Sisterhood including Li'l Meg.

"Would you like the coffee now?" Lola smiled at the men, apparently not intimidated by either their weapons or their angry looks.

"What do you think you are doing?" Master Duke snarled at Li'l Meg, ignoring the other women.

"You asked me to be your eyes and ears." She returned his stare.

Master Clint reached for his daughter. But before he could silence her, Lola said, "We know. We know Meg repeats everything we say back to you. That's how we knew you would join us today. Nothing we do is a secret from you."

"Take these troublemakers back to the *obanla's* compound," Master Duke commanded the men standing around the hall. "Malik can hold them until we conclude our business here."

As the men stepped forward, Marne noticed that Talé and her workers had disappeared into the warren of rooms behind the Market Board meeting room. She hoped they were able to escape.

The Demon Spawn grabbed the remaining members of the Sisterhood, Lola, Granny, Jumoke, Marne, and Anana. They pushed the women through the door and down the street, leaving Meg alone with Duke and Clint. How would Lola and the Sisterhood be able to oppose the Demon Spawn when they arrived tomorrow to fight for their expanded tribute? How would they stop the Hunters Guild from the dangerous resistance plans? Had Master Duke and his Spawn gang just neutralized the women's third way?

CHAPTER 19

When Lola, Gladys, Jumoke, Marne, and Anana along with their Demon Spawn guards arrived at the *obanla's* compound, the courtyard was overflowing with people. It looked to Marne as if everyone from the luncheon was there waiting for them to arrive. Both the Verdant Valley women and their Spawn guests were milling around, buzzing like an overturned beehive. The guards formed a circle around the women of the Sisterhood and pushed them toward the council chambers. Malik, wearing his white-on-white *agbada*, the formal robe he wore for public rituals, stood in the doorway.

"Duke said you are to retain these troublemakers," one of the guards said to Malik. "They are trying to disrupt our agreement."

The *obanla* picked Lola out from among the captive women. "Councilwoman Titilola," he said, using her formal name. "What is the meaning of this?"

Without warning, the mass of women in the courtyard began yelling and punching the guards. Marne could not hear what else was said between Malik and Lola but soon her group was hustled through the council chambers and into Malik's private meeting room.

The room was dark except for the lamp on the *obanla's* desk and the display hanging in the air above it.

"What have you done?" Malik asked turning to darken his display. "Where is Duke? Clint?"

Without answering Lola waved the women toward one of the small seating groups, taking the second most prominent chair for herself. As they settled themselves the women turned on the lights, so the area became an island of warmth in the darkness of the room. Malik appeared confused as he followed them. Marne thought of Master Duke's nickname for him, Milquetoast. Was he the ineffectual leader that name implied?

After seating himself in the remaining chair, Malik looked at the women.

"I'd like you to meet the Sisterhood of the Moon," Lola said, waving her hand to include all the women in her introduction. "I think you know everyone: Anana, your assistant…"

Malik frowned as if to ask Anana what she was doing with these rabble-rousers. Marne was proud of her friend for staring back at him instead of looking away as though embarrassed.

Lola continued, "Gladys and Jumoke, two of the senior women from the Market Board, and my assistant, Marne."

It wasn't the complete Sisterhood, of course. Marne had seen Talé among the women outside and, of course, they had left Meg with Clint and her father back at the Hall. She knew the Sisterhood's plan wouldn't work without those two women playing their parts outside.

"We have a plan for saving Verdant Valley from the demands of the Demon Spawn." Lola smiled.

Malik looked from one to another of the women, confusion and then anger racing across his face. "You what? Those men said you were prisoners of Master Duke, that you were fomenting some sort of disturbance. Based on the crowd outside I would say they were correct."

"We needed to talk to you. Since meetings are not allowed, this seemed like the best way." Lola looked pleased that their plan for talking to the *obanla* was working so well.

Malik glanced toward the main door to the room. As if on cue his assistant, Louis, poked his head in.

"Close and lock the door," Malik said before his chief of staff could question him. "Don't let anyone," his voice became stronger, "disturb us."

Without a word, Louis nodded and closed the door. Marne heard the click of the lock. There were other entrances to this room — the *obanla's* compound was a warren of passageways — but now they were somewhat protected from a direct assault.

Lola continued, "You remember when all this started, I brought my assistant Marne Abelabu to you." She nodded toward Marne. "We told you then that the Orisha did not support your plan to battle the Demon Spawn. But you refused to listen."

Malik opened his mouth as if to protest Lola's description of those events, but she didn't give him a chance to speak.

"Instead, you authorized the Hunters Guild to buy weapons and begin training. Then when Marne returned from the Demon Spawn encampment and told you about their preparations to overpower us, you refused to listen and assured Master Duke that his tribute would be ready." She stared at Malik as if daring him to contradict her. "You know and I know that the members of the Hunters Guild cannot defend us. They are police officers, not soldiers. And we both know that if you give the Spawn this second tribute not only will our people starve but you will be condemning the rest of the Reserve to starvation as well."

Malik stared at the wall behind Lola, apparently unwilling to either acknowledge or deny the truth of her statements.

"When you refused to stand up for our people, I gathered together a group of my artisans and market women. We have been formulating what we are calling a third way out of this dilemma. A strategy that forces us neither to submit to the Demon Spawn nor to fight a battle we are sure to lose."

The room was silent. Marne could hear the continued rumble of the women outside but inside no one moved, waiting for Malik to respond to Lola's statements.

"What have you done?" Malik whispered. "You know we cannot defy the Demon Spawn and now you have raised an army of women," his voice rose in disbelief, "an army of market women and artisans to defend us."

Before Lola could respond to Malik's lament, there was a pounding on the locked door. "Open up in there!" Master Clint's voice boomed into the room. Malik dropped his head into his hands, as though he was unable to face what was to come.

Lola nodded toward Anana. "Open the door before the brute breaks it in."

As soon as the door was unlocked, Master Clint slammed it open and marched into the room followed by his daughter. "Take her," he commanded.

Meg grabbed Marne's arm and pulled her to her feet. "He wants you," she whispered. "I couldn't stop him."

Marne pulled against Meg's grip, then looked toward Lola who only nodded. Marne realized she was going to play a bigger part in this than she had anticipated. When she looked at Master Clint he leered at her. Then he turned and followed Marne and Meg out of the room, slamming the door behind him.

"I want her protected," he told Meg as they stomped through the halls. "These people think they can defy Duke, but they don't know him. Take her back to her compound and keep her there."

He grabbed Marne, pulled her toward him and caressed her face. She shivered as the odor of dust and his manhood surrounded her. "Don't worry," he murmured. "Duke can't take what is mine."

The crowd of women in the courtyard quieted when Meg led Marne out of the council chambers, seated her on her cycle, and took her out of the compound.

Marne heard Master Clint behind them. "Out, Out," he told the women. "Go back to where you belong." His voice faded as they rode away.

"Clint is afraid for you." Meg's voice came though the speaker in Marne's helmet.

"He knows there's going to be carnage, if nothing's done," Marne said. She felt Meg's body tighten at the word *carnage*. They both knew that was where this confrontation was heading.

Without warning, Meg swung her cycle in a wide circle and they headed back toward where the women were shuffling out of the *obanla* compound. The high energy of the luncheon and the protest in the courtyard had dissipated. Taking off her helmet, Meg rode through the crowd yelling at the Demon Spawn women. Marne couldn't hear what was said but held up three fingers to remind the Verdant Valley women of the Sisterhood's third way. Perhaps all was not lost. Soon all the women were nodding and smiling again, moving with a new determination.

When Meg found Kandy Lynn and Talé walking together, she stopped and the three of them conferred. As Meg and Marne rode away from the crowd again, Meg's voice laughed in Marne's ear. "Duke thinks he's won this round, but we have another surprise for him."

Meg rode back through the streets and into Marne's compound. "Stay here," she said. "I'll be right back."

Still in shock from the events of the afternoon, Marne rested on the cycle. What was going to happen now? Most of the Sisterhood were being detained by Master Clint at the *obanla's* compound. It appeared that Meg and Talé had a backup plan, but Marne didn't see how they could move the third way ahead on their own. She still wasn't sure about Meg's loyalties, either.

In a few minutes Meg was back, wearing what Marne thought of as her full Demon Spawn regalia: black leather jacket and pants, boots, bandoliers crisscrossing her chest, and holstered guns on each hip. Meg and Marne left the compound and rode through some side streets. Soon they were headed toward the forest. Meg pulled off onto the road leading to a large open area the Hunters Guild sometimes used for their wrestling tournaments.

"Come on," she said, helping Marne from the cycle.

They walked toward the structure on the far side of the arena. Soon other cycles began to appear. Many of the Demon Spawn women brought a local woman with her. Meg and Marne, Kandy Lynn and Talé made their way up the steps of the pavilion. The others gathered around. Like Meg, all of the Demon Spawn women were wearing leather pants and jackets, bandoliers, and guns. They looked angry and mean. Marne was reminded of the first time she had seen the Demon Spawn at the council meeting. The day Master Clint had shot at Malik.

Meg raised her hands to quiet the crowd, but it was Kandy Lynn who stepped forward. Her face had begun to fill out in the short time she and her children had been in Verdant Valley and no longer looked like the waif

Marne had first met at the encampment. She held up one of the golden eggs Marne and Anana had given the women as they left the Market Hall. Throughout the crowd, women from both groups held up their own eggs.

"We are the Demon Spawn," Kandy Lynn said, her voice loud and strong. "We take what we want and don't look back. We have been taking our tribute from these people for many years. Under Junior's leadership, we were strong. When drought swept through the Republic, we didn't care, we always had enough for ourselves and our children. Every year the tribute came, and we were satisfied."

A murmur of agreement ran through the crowd.

"Now, Duke has changed everything. Every year my portion of the Verdant Valley tribute has been reduced. When I complained, Duke told me the weak must support the strong for the good of the whole. Every year he sells a portion our tribute to support his new militia. This year he plans on selling away the bulk of our tribute. Our fighters continued to be sleek and strong, but our children were starving."

Another murmur ran through the crowd.

"Duke says the people of the Reserve are rich. That they are fat while we are starving. So, this year he has demanded a second tribute. Where do you think that tribute will go? Into our children's stomachs? Or into the coffers of the Republic so Duke can buy more guns?"

"Guns," the Demon Spawn shouted. "More guns for everyone."

"Can our children eat guns? Can we?"

"No," the crowd roared. "We need food. Food. Food."

Kandy Lynn held up her hands again to quiet the crowd again.

"Who has given us food?" She shouted. "Has Duke given us food?"

"No," the crowd replied.

"Have Clint and his forces?"

"No."

Marne looked into the crowd and saw fear in the faces of the women from Verdant Valley. The Demon Spawn were getting more and more angry. When would they turn on their hosts and take what they wanted?

"Who," Kandy Lynn's softer voice silenced the crowd. "Who has fed us and our children?" She pulled Marne to her side. "This woman saw that my children were hungry and invited me here." She swept her arm over the crowd and pointed back toward the compounds. "These women shared their own food with us. It is these women who have pulled us back from starvation." She put her arm around Marne's waist and hugged her.

Then throughout the crowd Demon Spawn women hugged the Verdant Valley women standing near them.

"Thank you," Kandy Lynn whispered into Marne's ear. Then she turned back toward the crowd. "Tomorrow Duke and Clint expect to receive their second tribute but my new friend Talé tells me there is no second tribute. Instead some of the people of Verdant Valley have been preparing to defend their little town against us." Kandy Lynn paused. "Our forces will be able to win that battle and defeat the people of Verdant Valley. Duke and his forces may carry off all there is but..." she reached into a pocket and held up one of the golden eggs. "...we will return to our encampment empty-handed."

The crowd was silent. Everyone knew this confrontation was coming but no one had described it in such stark terms.

After her embrace of Marne, Kandy Lynn told the gang women to take their new friends back to their compounds and then return to the arena.

"This is Spawn business," Meg said when she brought Marne back to her courtyard. "We appreciate all that you have done for us, but this is going to get ugly."

As she watched Meg ride away, Marne wondered what she meant. The Sisterhood had hoped by recruiting Meg and welcoming the Demon Spawn women that they could recruit them into their third way plans. Now it appeared those plans were crushed. Lola and the rest of the Sisterhood were detained at the *obanla's* compound. Tomorrow Clint and his militia would destroy the people of Verdant Valley, take what they wanted, and leave the whole of the Babapupa Reserve to starvation.

Devastated by the turn of events, Marne trudged to her apartment. She felt like somehow she had disappointed Lola and her other sisters.

When she reached the apartment, she realized the door was unlocked. Fear flashed through her. Was Master Clint inside waiting for her? Would he be angry that she and Meg had gone out to the tournament grounds, instead of coming straight here? Had he finally come to claim her as his "hag"? What did that even mean?

Taking a deep breath, she sent a silent prayer to the Orisha and pushed the door open.

"About time." Anana's soft voice reached Marne moments before her arms encircled her. "Come on." Anana led Marne into the sitting room where Lola, her granny, and Jumoke were waiting.

Marne looked from one to the other. "How, how did you..." she stuttered. "I, I thought..." Anana pushed her toward a chair, then put a warm cup of tea in her hands.

Before the women could explain, there was a soft knock on the door. Marne cringed and pushed herself deeper into the corner of the sofa next to her godmother, Jumoke.

"Sorry I'm late," Talé's voice floated into the room. Anana stood up again, escorted her to the remaining chair, and handed her a cup of the tea.

"We convinced Malik and the rest of the council," Lola said. "How did it go with the Spawn?"

Talé took a sip of her tea. "Mmm, I needed that." She held the cup close to her face as though savoring the aroma. "Meg and Kandy Lynn have called a meeting of all the Demon Spawn out at the tournament grounds," she explained. "I passed Master Duke and the others on my way back." Talé took another sip of her tea. "I talked to Meg and Kandy Lynn before I left. They know what we're proposing, and I think they can get most of their women behind them. Now they need to convince their leaders and the other men to go along with our plan. We'll have to wait and see how it all works out, but I'm very hopeful."

"Harrumph," Marne's granny said. "If we can convince the Council and get the Hunters Guild to hold back, they should be able to do their part."

Marne had been impressed by Kandy Lynn's performance at the tournament grounds, but she wasn't sure she would be able stand up to Clint and Duke and all the other Spawn. She groaned and curled into a ball in the corner of the sofa. What would become of her when the Demon Spawn returned to carry off whatever they wanted?

Jumoke patted her arm. "Oh, sweetie. What's wrong?"

Marne curled up tighter. She had told these women how she had managed Master Clint at his encampment. She thought she had broken his obsession with her, but since she'd come home she realized he'd never let her return to her own life. He was determined to carry her back to his trailer and make her one of the Spawn. She felt the tears welling up in her eyes and creeping down her face.

Jumoke pulled Marne toward herself. "There, there," she murmured. "What's the matter?"

"Ma-Ma-Master Clint," Marne gasped, throwing herself onto Jumoke's shoulder.

Jumoke patted Marne's shoulder but let her cry as the other women made sympathetic murmurs.

When Marne's weeping had slowed to mere hiccups, Jumoke dipped a cloth into her tea and wiped Marne's face. "Now, sweetie, tell us what's wrong."

"Master Clint wants me. He's wanted me from the beginning. Master Duke called me Clint's plaything and told him to send me back here." She looked at the faces of the women who had formed the Sisterhood. She expected them to be scandalized, even disgusted. Instead they smiled and nodded, encouraging her to continue. "But you've seen how he is. No matter what, he's going to make me go with him." Her eyes filled with tears again.

Jumoke wiped the new tears from Marne's face. Now the cloth was cool and soothing. "Oh, sweetie," she said. "You've had a long day." Pulling Marne to her feet, Jumoke continued, "Let's you and me go give this to Yemaya. She won't let such an awful thing happen to you." She led her to the back of the apartment to Marne's small shrine.

The tiny room was almost dark, lit only by single over-sized candle hanging to the right of the large blue container set on a pedestal opposite the doorway. Other containers of different sizes and colors were scattered around the altar area. Marne threw herself down in front of the altar. She grabbed a nearby maraca and poured her heart out to the Orisha hiding in the blue vessel. Beginning with the first time she was Yemaya's principal speaker, she told the goddess everything she knew and had experienced in the last six weeks. She spoke of her hopes and fears as well as her triumphs and failures.

Jumoke squatted beside Marne, resting one hand on her shoulder while she prayed. When Marne finished, Jumoke stood and placed her hands on Marne's shoulders. "*A wa wa tow.*" She crossed her hands to touch the opposite shoulders. "*Yemaya, odide.*" She tapped Marne's shoulders to complete the blessing. When Marne stood up, Jumoke caught her in a hug and held her for a long time. Having emptied herself of all her fears, Marne felt a scrap of calm. Surely the Great Mother would not allow the Demon Spawn to take her again. She couldn't see how this confrontation between the Sisterhood and the gang would end, but she had put her trust in the Orisha and that was enough.

"Do you want to sleep in here tonight?" Jumoke asked, bringing Marne back to the present. When Marne nodded, her godmother disappeared, then returned carrying blankets and a pillow. "The rest of us are sleeping here as well," she said. "Perla has made up rooms for us. We need to stay together until this is over."

Marne lay down and let Jumoke tuck the blanket around her. After all that had happened and all that was yet to come, Marne doubted any of the Sisterhood would sleep tonight. However, before her godmother left the room she had slipped into oblivion.

CHAPTER 20

"Duke and Clint are gone." A singsong voice interrupted Marne's sleep. "Duke and Clint are gone. Wake up, sleepyhead. It's a new day."

When Marne heard Master Clint's name, she bolted upright. She was disoriented for a moment, forgetting that she had fallen asleep in front of her shrine.

"Is he here?" She looked around for an escape but knew there was none.

"No, silly." Anana squatted down beside her. "He's gone. They're both gone, left, run out."

"Run out?" Marne looked beyond her friend to see Jumoke and Lola smiling from the doorway. Had the entire Sisterhood spent the night in her apartment? Had they repelled Master Clint's efforts to abduct her again? Was that even possible?

"Come on." Anana pulled Marne to her feet. "We have great news."

Still only half awake, Marne stumbled into the sitting room where the rest of the Sisterhood waited for her. Even Meg was there, still dressed in her black leather jacket and pants. A damp rag covered the right side of her face. With the extreme care of someone for whom every move was painful, Meg lowered her hand and leaned forward to grasp the mug on the table in front of her. As she took a sip of coffee, Marne saw a nasty bruise had bloomed on one cheek and her right eye was swollen shut. The Yemaya stone Jumoke had given her was resting on her chest.

Her movements slow and deliberate, Meg looked exhausted but satisfied somehow. The other women were smiling as though they had won a great victory.

Jumoke pressed a cup of steaming coffee into Marne's hands and led her to the sofa where she had cowered in fear last night. Marne looked toward the entrance, expecting Master Clint to be waiting for her, but no one was there. She sat down, pulling her legs under her. She wanted to make herself as small as possible, as if that would protect her from him.

The women sat and sipped their coffee, waiting for Marne to become fully awake.

Then Lola got up and stood behind Meg. "I'd like you to meet the new leader of the Demon Spawn." Meg grimaced as Lola put her hands on her shoulders and the rest of the women clapped.

Marne looked from one to the other of the women, confused.

"When we left the tournament grounds last night," Talé began, "we knew the Spawn women were planning some sort of insurrection. Apparently, Meg and Kandy Lynn convinced all the Spawn that Duke had been defrauding them. He was using our tribute and their other proceeds for his own benefit. As I understand what happened, it wasn't easy…"

More awake now, Marne noticed there was muddy residue in the seams of Meg's clothes, as if she had been rolling around on in the dirt.

"In the end," Talé said, "they eliminated Duke and exiled Clint. They're gone."

"A small group of his militia went with Clint. The rest accepted Meg as their new leader." Jumoke patted Marne's knee. "He's gone."

"Gone?" Marne looked from one to another of the women, ending with Meg. "Your father left?"

Meg nodded, reaching up to caress the Jumoke's turquoise kingmaker stone.

Meg looked so stern, Marne felt a shiver of fear race down her spine. "Where?"

"A group of my people are escorting Duke's body, Clint, and the others back to the encampment," Meg said. "They'll help them clear out his things. By tomorrow he and his rabble have to be outside our territory. They could try to join a gang south of the City, but I expect they'll go over to Washitonia or maybe Texarkana. I don't know for sure. But they're not coming back here. I promise."

Relief flooded through Marne. Master Clint was gone. He wasn't coming back for her. Perhaps her nightmare was over.

"But there's more." Lola nodded toward Talé, who still stood with her hands on Meg's shoulders.

"The Demon Spawn have a new leader." Talé beamed as though announcing a promotion among her own staff. "Meg is in charge now. And Kandy Lynn is her assistant."

"Meg?" Marne uncurled herself as Meg smiled at her. "You're the new leader of the Demon Spawn? How? When?"

"Last night," Meg said, her serious expression returning. "In the end, the gang turned against Duke and Clint and now they're gone. It wasn't easy." She touched her swollen cheek. "No one died except Duke. And it may not last, but for now I am our leader. Kandy Lynn is my second."

Marne shook her head. Last night Clint had said he was coming for her and now he was gone. Duke, too. And Meg, Li'l Meg, was in charge?

Talé returned to her seat as Jumoke moved around the room refilling everyone's coffee cups. When she returned to the sofa, she pulled Marne toward her, enveloping her in a comforting embrace.

Lola cleared her throat. "Meg's new position puts her in a unique position as both the leader of the Demon Spawn and a member of this Sisterhood." She nodded toward Meg, who winced. "Members of her people are still poised to take at least a portion of Duke's second tribute by force if necessary. They are starving, after all."

Meg nodded. Marne realized that even if the Demon Spawn understood Talé's story of the Golden Egg there were other forces at work.

"And," Lola said, "we have the Hunters Guild armed and prepared to defend us."

Marne remembered her vision of blood filling the Market Hall. She shuddered.

Jumoke pulled Marne tighter as Lola continued, "Now, we need to plan our next moves."

Meg put her coffee cup on the table. "I shouldn't be here." She stood up, slowed by her injuries.

"No," Talé said. "We got this far by working together. Please hear what we have to offer."

Meg looked around the room. The older women nodded. "Please stay," Marne's granny said. "We need you to help us find a way that works for your people and for ours."

Shaking her head, Meg slid back into the chair. "This is a bad idea," she muttered.

"*Tutu Eleggua*," Lola muttered, invoking the Orisha who opened and closed the doors of communication. "While you were out at the tournament grounds with Talé and Marne last night, Jumoke, Gladys, Anana, and I met with the *obanla*. When you called Duke, Clint, and the rest of your people away we held an emergency meeting of the village council."

Meg scowled. Meetings of the Council in the absence of their Demon Spawn shadows had been forbidden since Master Duke first invaded their chambers almost a month ago.

"The Council agreed to meet with leaders of the Spawn," Lola nodded toward Meg, "— that's you now — to work out a new agreement. An agreement that prevents disaster for both our peoples. They said if you agreed, they would accept members of the Sisterhood as mediators. Not everyone, of course. You would be leading the Demon Spawn delegation. Marne, Anana, and I are still part of the Council and its staff. But Gladys and Jumoke as the elders of the Sisterhood can convene the meeting and help lead us to a satisfactory compromise. And Talé, since she knows the status of our harvest."

Marne looked from Lola to the two older women to Meg and back. Meg's frown softened as she considered Lola's proposal. She opened and shut her mouth several times as though preparing some sort of counter-proposal. Finally, she nodded. "I want Kandy Lynn and a couple others with me."

Lola nodded.

"Then we agree." Meg leaned back in her chair still holding the cloth against her injured face. "Tell me what you have in mind."

Marne and Anana followed Malik the *obanla*, Raymon his *baala*, and Lola as they left the *obanla's* compound and walked around the corner toward the village square.

After their early morning meeting with Meg and the rest of the Sisterhood, Lola and Talé, together with Marne and Anana, had returned to the council offices in the *obanla's* compound. Having convinced the village council to accept their plan for negotiating with the Demon Spawn the night before, Lola and Talé had spent the rest of this morning with the Council to make arrangements. Now the three council members were on their way to the Hunters Guild Hall to convince the Guild to forgo their planned attack on the Spawn, cache their new weapons, and resume their duties as the guardians of the social order. Lola had insisted the two assistants, Marne and Anana, accompany them.

As they made their way through the square, Marne remembered her visit to the Guild with Akande and the detour they had made to one of the benches scattered around the area. She shivered as she remembered his seduction almost a month ago and her later kidnapping by Master Clint. She was no longer the innocent girl she had been at the end of the summer and she wondered about her life after the upcoming negotiations. She had escaped Clint, and Lola had promised to protect her from Akande, but she was still uncertain about her future.

Damola, the Hunters Guild's *baala* and Hackett's second-in-command, opened the door of the hall when Malik knocked. Like many members of the Guild, Damola was a muscular man who moved with a subtle air of authority. Dressed in the traditional Hunters Guild uniform of denim pants and a leather vest over a sparkling white shirt, his frown and cold manner suggested he was not pleased at the Council's decision.

"Malik, Raymon, Lola," he nodded at the council members, "welcome."

Lola stepped forward. "Thank you for agreeing to meet with us. I believe you know our assistants, Anana and Marne?"

Without acknowledging the younger women, Damola stepped aside and allowed them to enter the hall lobby. Each member of Malik's party stopped in front of the Warrior's shrine and made a small offering. Where the Market Board's entrance shrine featured Eleggua, this one also included the warrior Orisha and patrons of the Guild, Ogun and Ochosi. Dominating the display was an iron kettle filled with one full-sized and several smaller swords, farm tools, deadly-looking arrows, and a heavy iron chain. Praying for the success of the Sisterhood's mission, Marne dipped her hand into the basin of cool water and sprinkled it onto the Orisha's tools, cooling their implied heat. As she followed Lola and the others through another doorway, she heard someone slam the outer door of the hall shut.

The main hall of the Hunters Guild building was similar to that of the Market Board. A large altar filled with more of Ogun's and Ochosi's tools was built into an alcove on the left side of the room. As in the Market Board's meeting room, the chairs were arranged in a series of concentric semicircles around a central open area, with special chairs for the Guild chairperson and his assistants placed in the opening between the two ends of the circles. There were also places for the *obanla* and his party.

Most of the seats were already filled with the members of the Guild. As soon as Malik and his people found their places, Hackett and Damola, the *baala*, walked over to the Ogun altar. Flicking water toward the altar, Hackett chanted, "*Omi Tutu, Ani Tutu, Ile Tutu, Egun Tutu, Laroye Tutu, Aiku Baba Wa.*" Marne translated in her head. May cool water bless us. May a cool road lead us. May cool relatives surround us. May a cool house envelop us. May cool Ancestors watch over us. May the owner of gossip never lead us astray. May the ancestors bring their blessings to us.

Damola picked up a bell and rang it as Hackett continued to pray. Finally, Hackett called, "*Ashé*" and the people in the room echoed, "*Ashé.*" So be it.

After the two men returned to their chairs, Hackett introduced Malik's party and summarized the results of the council meeting the night before. "Against my better judgment, I have agreed to allow Lola and her so-called Sisterhood attempt to negotiate with the Demon Spawn. We will stand down long enough for them to change the course of events."

The room exploded. Marne heard, "No!" "Suicide." "…Evil!"

Damola pounded a heavy metal staff, the emblem of his office, on the floor until order was restored. "Sit down and listen to Hackett," he commanded, his deep voice regaining control of the room.

"I invited Malik and these others here to help us to understand the Council's decision," Hackett continued, "but we can't hear them if you all talk at once." He turned toward Malik, who deferred to Lola as if to say, "this is yours, you deal with it."

Lola stood and walked to the shrine, where she sprinkled water on Ogun's tools, then returned to the front of the Guild members.

"A month ago, Malik and I brought my assistant," she nodded toward Marne, "to you. She told you that the Demon Spawn were preparing an overwhelming force against us. I told you then that I was working with a group of my market women to find another solution to this problem. As I told you then, the Sisterhood of the Moon, as we called ourselves, invited the women and children of the Demon Spawn who were starving to come as visitors to our compounds. I'm sure you've all noticed the increased number of *oyinbo* in your compounds." She paused long enough to give the Guild members time to take in what she was saying.

"Two days ago, the Market Board held its first Harvest Festival. At that luncheon we were able to share our dilemma with our Spawn guests. As a result, last night the gang ousted Duke and Clint and choose a new leader — Clint's daughter, the one known as Li'l Meg." Again, Lola paused long enough to let her words sink in.

Marne glanced toward Akande. What was he thinking? Had he really been planning something with Master Clint, the Demon Spawn enforcer?

"Meg and the other leaders of the Spawn are willing to work out a new agreement with us," Lola continued. "The Council has accepted our proposal and now we need the Guild to set aside their plans to defend us and work with the Council and the Sisterhood."

Again the room exploded with shouted questions. Damola stood up and again thumped his staff on the floor. But before order could be restored, with a roar, one of the Guild members bounded over the chairs. The man had kicked off his shoes and torn away his leather jacket and the shirt beneath. He crouched bare-chested and barefooted in the open area in front of Hackett, Damola, and Malik's delegation. He carried a deadly-looking sword in one hand and a heavy metal chain in the other. By the vacant look in his eyes, Marne recognized that the Orisha Ogun, patron of the Guild, had entranced one of his speakers in order to join the meeting.

Grabbing a gourd shaker from the altar behind him, Damola approached the Orisha, shaking the maraca at him and singing to him in the ritual language. Someone in the crowd started clapping Ogun's drum rhythm, which got picked up by others in the room.

"*Eje. Eje,*" the Orisha said, stomping around the center of the crescent of chairs.

Blood, blood, Marne translated to herself. As she watched the Orisha begin swinging the chain over the heads of the assembled crowd, she thought of her own visit from Yemaya at the Market Board meeting almost a month ago. She remembered her vision of blood everywhere. Had this speaker seen a similar vision? No one had wanted to listen to her then. Would they listen to Ogun's speaker now?

Alternating his chant of *eje* with *iku,* death, the Orisha swung the lethal chain over the people's heads while brandishing the sword near their throats. Only the *baala* approached him, shaking the maraca, singing, and stomping. Everyone in the room sat perfectly still. Marne wondered whether they were afraid of what the Orisha might do. Ogun the owner of all weapons could be dangerous. Round and round he circled, threatening individuals and groups while the crowd clapped his rhythm and Damola attempted to gain control.

Then without warning, the Orisha collapsed to the floor, screaming and weeping. Damola signaled to Hackett, who handed him the bowl of water from the altar. Singing more softly, the *baala* splashed water on top of Ogun's head and the back of his neck. The clapping continued, but slower and more muffled. As the Orisha calmed, the *baala* took the sword and chain from His hands and gave them to members of the Guild who returned them to the entrance shrine.

Still speaking the ritual language, the *baala* questioned the Orisha. Marne couldn't hear what was being said but it was obvious Ogun had an opinion about the meeting. He looked around the room until he found Malik and his delegation. Nodding to the Council members, the speaker appeared to pass out. Damola motioned to a couple of the Guild members, who helped the dazed man to his feet and led him away.

As the speaker was taken from the room, the clapping slowed, then stopped. The *baala* stood up and stumbled back to the altar where he replaced the maraca and bowl of water. Then he lay prostrate on the mat in front of the altar. Marne could see he was panting as though exhausted. Hackett splashed water on the top of his head and the back of his neck, then helped him stand up and return to his chair.

Hackett bowed to the altar. "*Modupue*, Ogun," he said loud enough for everyone in the room to hear.

"*Modupue*," the room echoed. Thank you.

No one spoke until the speaker and his helpers returned. The man looked exhausted and still a little stunned.

"...'Twas Ogun who, after storing water in abundance in his house, then proceeded to have a bath of blood...'" The *baala* quoted from a popular hymn to Ogun. "I now ask: 'Where is Ogun to be found? Ogun is found where there is a fight. Ogun is found where there is vituperation. Ogun is found where there are torrents of blood...'"

Everyone in the room seemed to be holding his breath.

Then Damola continued, "Ogun says that you are picking a fight you cannot win. Ogun predicts a deluge of blood if you continue down this path. Ogun weeps for all his sons and daughters who will be no more."

Marne looked at the speaker, who dropped his head onto his knees. She wondered again whether, like her, he had seen a bloody flood filling the room.

The *baala* looked toward Malik and his delegation. "Ogun says only those who have joined together in sisterhood can prevent disaster."

For a long moment, no one responded. Then Hackett nodded to Lola. "Tell us what we must do."

CHAPTER 21

Two days after Marne awoke to her new reality without the threat of Master Clint, she was seated behind Lola in the *obanla*'s ceremonial hall. Today the Verdant Valley council was negotiating a new arrangement with Meg and the Demon Spawn. Getting everyone to this meeting had tested the leadership skills of the members of the Sisterhood and their Demon Spawn allies. Two nights ago, while the Demon Spawn were out at the arena, Lola had convinced Malik, Akande, and the rest of the Council that negotiation was a viable option. Once the Council was convinced, the Hunters Guild had to be persuaded to forgo their planned belligerent response to the Demon Spawn's demands. Only after Ogun, the patron of the Guild, withdrew his support and predicted a bath of blood for them and their families, did the Guild throw their support behind the Sisterhood. Lola, with Malik and his *baala* Raymon, had convinced the Guild members to cache their weapons and resume their duties as the guardians of the social order.

At the same time that Lola was talking to the Guild, Meg, Kandy Lynn, and the Demon Spawn women had to persuade their own militia that the planned looting would destroy the village they had come to depend on. Apparently "Don't kill the goose that lays the golden egg" had become those women's rallying cry, referring to the story Marne had never heard before Harvest Festival but perfectly described the situation from the women's viewpoint.

Coaxing both the Demon Spawn leaders with their militia, the Verdant Valley council, and the Hunters Guild to accept the wisdom of the Sisterhood's third way had at first appeared impossible. Yet here they were, gathered in a single room to negotiate their combined futures.

Looking around, Marne was relieved when it appeared Meg had been able to convince her people to leave their guns and bandoliers behind.

"I'll do what I can," she had told Lola and the others, "but you need to realize I can't remove all their hidden weapons. They won't be completely unarmed."

If the Hunters Guild members were also armed, in spite of the demands of Ogun and their leadership, it wasn't obvious.

Some of the Demon Spawn women had brought their own weapons — their children. Marne was glad to see that in just the short time since these women and children had been in Verdant Valley, they were looking healthier. Their cheeks were not as gaunt, and the children were quicker to laugh and talk. In spite of all the work Lola and the Sisterhood had done to bring the meeting about, it was these women with their wide-eyed children who had convinced their husbands and fathers to attend.

The noise of people jostling for seats and discussing this unusual event made it impossible for Marne to do more than smile at Anana, who sat behind the *obanla*. Since there was no other hall big enough for everyone who wanted to attend this meeting, Malik had opened his formal ceremonial hall.

During the winter ritual season this space would be extravagantly decorated in the colors of the Orisha with an abundance of altars and performance areas. Today, however, it had been left plain and unadorned, except for the altar the Sisterhood had built along the wall opposite the entrance. Although Oya, the patron of the Market Board, held the place of honor, all the Orisha were represented there, watching over the proceedings.

In the hall, chairs were set up in concentric semicircles around a central open area where three tables were arranged in a triangle. Meg, Kandy Lynn, and two men Marne didn't recognize, still dressed in their black leather jackets and pants, but without their weapons, sat on one side of the triangle. When she saw Meg's black-and-blue cheek and swollen eye, Marne wondered whether she still wore her kingmaker stone beneath her shirt. Malik, Akande, and Lola from the village council sat on the second side, along with a representative of *Obanla* Joseph, leader of the entire Babapupa Reserve and the great *obanla* of its capital city, Scarlet Dawn. Visitors from several other villages and the rest of the village council with their aides and assistants, including Anana and Marne, sat behind them. Marne's granny and Jumoke, who would serve as mediators and facilitators of this gathering, sat on the third side of the triangle. Talé was with them. As the manager of High Valley Fields, the largest agricultural complex in the valley, she was most familiar with the old tribute agreement and their current harvests.

Everyone from Verdant Valley was dressed in their most dignified clothing. Malik and the other men on the council were in *agbadas*, the traditional flowing wide-sleeved robe worn for formal and ritual occasions, while the women on the council and at the mediator's table wore traditional wrappers and head-ties.

Beyond the working group were chairs for the people of Verdant Valley and the Demon Spawn to attend as observers. Much of the crowd spilled out the open doors and into the village square where loudspeakers were set up for them. Members of the Hunters Guild, in their denim trousers and leather vests, were stationed strategically around the room and in the square, prepared to keep order if any of those in attendance got unruly.

When everyone was finally settled down, Jumoke picked up the gourd of water from the altar and carried it to the front door. They could all hear her chanting: "*Omi Tutu, Ona Tutu, Ani Tutu, Ile Tutu, Egun Tutu, Laroye Tutu, Aiku Baba Wa.*" May cool water bless you. May a cool road lead you. May cool relatives surround you. May a cool house envelop you. May cool Ancestors watch over you. May the owner of gossip never lead you astray. May the ancestors bring their blessings to you.

The meeting had begun.

Marne's granny stood up. She raised her arms to encompass the entire room. "Thank you all for attending this historic meeting. My name is Gladys Abelabu. With me is Jumoke Finley. As members of the Sisterhood of the Moon, we have been asked to mediate this discussion."

Turning toward the table of Babapupa officials, she said, "I want to welcome *Obanla* Malik, members of the Verdant Valley council, and Ernest Iles, who brings us greetings from *Obanla* Joseph." Lola had told Marne Ernest was the chief diviner of the Scarlet Dawn council. Now he and Lola smiled and nodded toward the women, even though Malik and Akande stared straight ahead, refusing to acknowledge the introduction.

Gesturing toward the Demon Spawn table, Gladys continued, "Joining us also are Maggie Sue Sapulpa, the newly elected leader of the Spawn, along with her assistant Kandy Lynn Wentworth and..." She nodded toward Meg, who waved her off, not introducing the other members of her group.

It appeared the tough woman who had first invaded the meetings of the Sisterhood had returned. Again, Meg looked intimidating in her black leather clothing. Then Marne noticed Meg slide her palm down to rest on her belly. Meg had more than her status as the leader of the Spawn to protect. Marne wondered whether one of the two men sitting with Meg was the father of her child. Was he aware?

"As many of you may know, there has been an agreement between the Verdant Valley council and members of the Demon Spawn that we would provide a tribute yearly to the Demon Spawn as payment for their protection."

Marne wondered what the Demon Spawn were protecting them from and who had been protecting them from the Spawn. Not Malik and the council.

"Before we begin a discussion of the problems with this year's tribute, I've asked Talé Williford, the manager of High Valley Fields, to explain how the tribute has been working. Talé?"

As Talé stood up, several people dressed not in the formal clothing of the rest of the group but in grubby farm clothes stepped out of the crowd and piled baskets along the inner edge of the mediators table. It appeared that the baskets were full of golden eggs similar to those Marne and Anana had given to the Demon Spawn women and children after the Harvest Festival meeting.

"Thank you, Gladys." Talé walked to an opening between the negotiator's and Verdant Valley tables so she could stand in the middle of the triangle. She gestured toward the baskets. "These represent the harvest of all the farms in the Reserve. Based on our past agreement we've been giving about fifteen percent of our harvest to Demon Spawn." She picked up about a sixth of the baskets and set them in front of Meg and Kandy Lynn. Then she began piling baskets in front of Ernest. "Much of the rest was sold to the other villages of the Reserve."

While she was talking, a couple of *oyinbo* men in business suits reached between Meg and Kandy Lynn and took all but one of their baskets, leaving a large knife in their place.

Ignoring the Demon Spawn, Talé divided the remaining baskets into two groups. The workers put a sign reading "Verdant Valley" by one set of baskets and one with "Seeds" by the other. "We kept the remainder for ourselves and to plant the following spring," she said. "In the past, we were able to sell some of our crops to the Republic, but for the last several years our harvest has been down. Now we are living year-to-year, hoping the rains return soon." A sign reading "Republic of the Southwest" was set on the table away from any of the baskets. She nodded toward Marne's granny and Jumoke, then returned to her seat.

In the silence that followed, Marne noticed Meg, Kandy Lynn, and the others at the Demon Spawn table staring at the baskets piled in front of Ernest, the representative from the Reserve. Even though Lola and the Sisterhood had already worked out the beginning of a solution with Meg, Marne wondered whether she and her people thought they should have a portion of that allocation. Perhaps they didn't realize that was all the food for the rest of Babapupa Reserve. Did they understand yet there was no surplus they could draw from? No hidden stockpile? Would the Sisterhood's carefully crafted third way actually save them?

Lola stood up and looked over the baskets spread between the three tables. "A month ago, Master Duke and other members of the Demon

Spawn came to the council demanding we pay them a second tribute. We didn't know it at the time, but the last couple of years the leaders of the Spawn have been selling much of what we sent them to the Republic to buy weapons." She gestured toward the single basket and the knife remaining in front of Meg. "Because their people, especially their women and children, were hungry the Demon Spawn wanted more from us." She waved at the baskets scattered between the three tables. "But as you can see, Verdant Valley doesn't have more to give them. The Hunters Guild prepared to defend what little we had. Understanding that no one would win such a battle, the Sisterhood of the Moon was formed to find a third way out of this crisis. That brings us to today."

Lola paused and looked around the room. "Members of the Sisterhood have met with the village council, including the representative from Babapupa, and with Meg, Kandy Lynn, and some of their people. We have reached certain preliminary agreements that I want to reiterate now." Lola nodded, and a large screen popped into existence behind her. Marne knew there were similar screens outside for those who couldn't get into the hall.

"We all understand that we are working with a finite harvest. There is not any more to be had from our stores. The Demon Spawn and the Reserve may be able to acquire additional food from the Republic but there is a region-wide drought and additional food is unlikely." Lola nodded and the words "Finite Harvest" appeared on the screen. Marne looked around and saw Halima, the *baala* of the Market Board, holding a controller for the projector.

"Number two, we cannot dip into our seed stores. It is important that the Reserve farmers, Talé and others, can plant in the spring. We will not kill the goose that supports all of us." The words "Preserve Seed Stores" appeared on the screen.

"And three," Lola reached down and caught Kandy Lynn's daughter who ran behind her. She balanced the child on her hip. "And three, no one should go hungry. Everyone has agreed that even the weakest will share in whatever is decided." The words "No One Goes Hungry" appeared on the screen.

Everyone was quiet, staring at the screen. They had come to the impasse. Meeting Lola's three requirements appeared impossible.

Anana walked to the mediator's table and took the *oyinbo* child from Lola's arms. She looked toward the Demon Spawn. "When Marne returned from the Demon Spawn encampment," Anana said, "she told us that their women and children were starving because their leaders had sold the food we gave them to buy weapons."

Anana frowned at Meg and the other Demon Spawn. "I suggested we could invite them here. Kandy Lynn has tried to explain it to me, but I still don't understand how the Demon Spawn could let their women and children go hungry. My compound and I fed Kandy Lynn and her children when their own people would not." She kissed the child's cheek, then handed her to another woman from Marne and Anana's family. "Other women did the same when more Demon Spawn women came to Verdant Valley."

Anana looked around the room at the cluster of Demon Spawn men and women. Scowling, she returned to her seat.

Marne could see that Lola was ready to make the Market Board's offer. Looking at the baskets arranged on the three tables, Marne realized that it wouldn't be enough. They couldn't feed the Demon Spawn, themselves, and the whole rest of the Reserve.

Before Lola could speak, one of the *oyinbo* men whispered something in Meg's ear. His black leather jacket and pants were dusty as though he'd just ridden in from some distant location. She stood up. Marne could tell she was still sore from whatever happened the night she had gained her new position. Watching her, Marne wondered how the Meg had defeated Clint and Duke.

"If we could have a moment," Kandy Lynn said, watching Meg follow the man toward the back of the room. "I believe we might have some new information."

Nodding, Lola sat down. While they waited, Marne tried to guess which of the two men sitting at the Demon Spawn table might be the father of Meg's child. One was a big angry-looking man with dark curly hair and watery-blue eyes. His skin had a ruddy undertone as though he had been out in the sun too long. Marne was surprised that his hands were almost as dark as her own. Then she realized his were covered with an oily residue that had seeped into all the wrinkles and ridges. Early in the summer, when she had time to flirt with the boys in the market, she met one with hands like that. It seemed like a lifetime ago. Her friend was a mechanic out at Talé's farm. She remembered that no matter how much he scrubbed, he could never get his hands clean. Perhaps the Demon Spawn man was also a mechanic.

The other man was thinner, not as mean looking. He projected a display on the table in front of him. All through Talé's presentation he had poked at it, as if trying to verify her account. Now he turned to Kandy Lynn and showed her his findings. She frowned and nodded. Perhaps they finally realized there was no way the Demon Spawn could increase the Verdant Valley harvest.

Meg returned to stand behind her chair. The man in the dusty clothes stood with her. She looked toward Marne. "Some of you will be pleased to know that Clint and his friends have left our encampment and are headed toward Texarkana."

Marne sighed. She had been so afraid the deposed Demon Spawn leader would invade this meeting and force her to go with him. But he was truly gone. The snake in her stomach began to uncoil. Perhaps Meg really had put an end to the horror of Clint's intentions for her.

"I'm also told that only a small portion of this year's tribute has already been sold. The rest is still in our mountain warehouse. We are not as destitute as we thought."

A cheer of "Meg, Meg," rippled through the hall and out into the plaza beyond.

Meg waved her hand. Marne thought she would be happy, but she looked angry.

"For some time now, I have had to endure people telling me that the Demon Spawn steal from each other." She looked toward the mediators' table and frowned but before the crowd could react, she continued. "And it was true. But that stops now." She gestured toward those sitting with her. "Kandy Lynn, Billy Ray, Otis, and I will see that we provide for our own — the strong and the weak."

The room exploded in another long, loud cheer.

She sat down but she wasn't finished speaking. "Many years ago, Junior made an agreement with the Verdant Valley council. If they shared a portion of their harvest with us, we would protect their people from the other gangs. Today we're ready to renegotiate a fair exchange, one that protects your people and ours." She nodded toward the Verdant Valley table.

Sitting behind the council table, Marne couldn't see the reaction of the Verdant Valley delegates, but she knew the negotiations would be much easier now.

Finally, Malik stood up. "Congratulations," he said, nodding toward the Demon Spawn delegation. "We certainly want to continue our relationship with our Demon Spawn friends."

Marne wondered whether the other people in the room heard the sarcasm in his voice.

"As we discussed before this meeting," the *obanla* continued, "returning to a percentage of our harvest seems like an honorable way of working together in these uncertain times." He waved toward the basket of golden eggs on all three tables. "As you can see, this year's harvest has been distributed. We're pleased that you found so much of your tribute, that means everyone will have food for the coming year. However, the members of our Market Board are still concerned about the weakest members of the Demon Spawn, the women and children who have been underfed for the past several years."

Meg frowned, then opened her mouth as if to object.

Without giving Meg an opportunity to say anything, Malik turned toward Lola, "I'll let council member Titilola tell you about their offer. Lola?"

Lola stood up again. She glared at Meg and the other Demon Spawn. "It was a wretched day for us when you and your father decided to kidnap my young assistant, Marne Abelabu, and take her back to your encampment."

Meg's face hardened as she returned Lola's stare.

"But it was a fortunate day for you," Lola continued. "While she was there Marne saw the appalling conditions of your people and met Kandy Lynn and her children."

Kandy Lynn caught Marne's eye and the two young women nodded at each other.

"When Kandy Lynn came to visit us, it began a new phase in the relationship between the people of Verdant Valley and the Demon Spawn. Kandy Lynn was soon followed by other hungry women and their children and my market women found places for them in their compounds." Applause broke out among the Demon Spawn women and spread through the hall.

"Thank you." Lola nodded toward the audience, acknowledging their appreciation. "We only did what was right." She walked through the opening between the tables and stood in front of the Demon Spawn delegation. "Now that you have found most of our original tribute is unsold, you have assured us that the weakest among you will be provided for."

Meg nodded while continuing to scowl at Lola. It was obvious she hadn't known about this portion of the meeting.

Lola picked up one of the golden eggs from the Demon Spawn baskets. "At our Harvest Festival, we gave everybody one of these golden eggs to remind you that while we have given freely to you, there was a limit to what we could give." She bounced the egg in her hand giving everyone a chance to remember and to remind each other of the story of the goose that laid the golden egg.

When the murmuring quieted, she continued. "Now the members of my Market Board want all of you to know that we will continue to support you and your children. We pledge to open the doors of our compounds to anyone who comes to us with one of these eggs. We don't have an infinite surplus, but we will share what we have with those in need." She handed the egg to Kandy Lynn, then turned and walked back to her seat among the Verdant Valley delegation.

More murmurs ran through the crowd. Marne could hear people asking each other what Lola meant.

Finally, Lola stood up again and reached into the basket in front of her. "What I'm saying is simple, no one should go hungry. This egg is our pledge that we'll do what we can to help our Demon Spawn friends, especially their women and children."

Lola tossed the egg across the triangle toward Meg, who reached out at the last moment and caught it. She stared at the egg, then looked up, her anger gone. "Thank you," she said. "You and your women have become good friends to me and mine."

CHAPTER 22

So much had happened and so much had changed. After their meeting mere days ago, the council and the leaders of the Spawn had formulated a new agreement. Then Meg and her people returned to their encampment carrying away the golden eggs that were the Market Board's pledge to them.

Marne was exhausted from the emotions of the past month. Had it really only been six weeks since Duke and Clint had invaded the Verdant Valley council meeting? Working for Lola and the council had seemed like a simple break from her work among the dye pots. But it had become so much more and she wanted out of her agreement with Lola.

This morning Marne had asked to meet with her and now the two of them were in the council woman's sitting room sharing a cup of coffee. She sat on the sofa while Lola was in one of the chairs. A small table between them held the pot.

"I'm sorry. I just can't continue." Marne looked into Lola's face. Her boss had aged over these past weeks.

"Working for the council isn't usually so intense, you know," Lola smiled at her.

Marne nodded. She knew dealing with the Demon Spawn, forming the Sisterhood, and devising their third way had added unique pressures to Lola's work.

"Perhaps you'd find the work boring," Lola said, smiling, "after everything that's happened."

Marne shook her head, and then pressed ahead with the speech she had prepared. "I appreciate the opportunity you've given me by asking me to be your assistant, but Granny has recruited the rest of her assistants. They're firing up her dye pots next week and that's where I want to be."

She didn't mention that since Meg and the Demon Spawn had returned to their encampment, Akande had been leering at her again. He hadn't done or said anything yet, but she felt like it was only a matter of time before he would find a way to be alone with her again. In spite of her success in dealing with Master Clint, she wasn't confident she could fend off Akande's advances. And, apparently, Lola couldn't stop him either.

"If you'd let me work at the shop again next summer, I'd love that, but I don't want to come to the *obanla's* compound anymore." Marne looked at the disappointment on Lola's face, then dropped her eyes to her hands, neatly folded in her lap.

Lola set her cup on the table and moved to sit next to Marne. "I know Gladys will be happy to get started on her work and I know she'll keep you busy." She dropped her arm over Marne's shoulder and pulled her close. "You've become like a daughter to me and I want you to do what makes you happy." She squeezed Marne in a light hug and then returned to her chair.

Tears filled Marne's eyes. She realized she loved Lola, too.

The councilwoman sat staring over Marne's head for a long time. Would she refuse to let her assistant leave? Would Marne be able to defy her if she did?

Lola nodded as if making a decision. "I'll borrow one of Malik's assistants until I can hire someone. Come to me in the spring and we'll work out your duties for the summer season."

Marne released the breath she had not even realized she was holding. Lola was going to let her leave now and come back to the shop in the spring.

Lola stood up. "Now, show me what you've been working on and then you can leave, free to continue learning the dyer's art."

Marne stood up and the two of them went to the assistant's small office. Marne had spent the day finishing up her work and organizing things so when she left today she would leave for good.

After they finished going over her work, Lola walked Marne to the *obanla's* office.

When Louis let them in, the *obanla* was sitting at his desk. Marne thought he looked older, too. He stood to greet them.

"Marne won't be continuing with us," Lola told him. "The council owes her a great debt. Without her sacrifice and work we never would have been able to pacify the Demon Spawn."

"Yes, yes." Malik appeared distracted. "You've done us a great service. Thank you. Louis will see that you receive appropriate compensation." He turned away, back to whatever he was working on. If Lola was hoping for more, she was disappointed.

The two women walked to the entrance of the council offices. "Enjoy your time with Gladys and come see me about next spring." Lola pulled Marne into a hug.

Before they could say more, Anana came up behind them. "Are you going home?" she asked. Marne nodded. "Then come along. I'll walk with you." She slipped her arm through Marne's and led her across the courtyard and out the gate of the *obanla's* compound. Marne didn't look back to see whether anyone was watching. She had never been so relieved to be leaving a compound. She hoped she'd never have to get involved in politics again.

ABOUT THE AUTHOR

Mary Ann Clark is both a published scholar and an explorer of speculative fiction.

Growing up on the high plains of Colorado, Mary Ann received her undergraduate degree from Creighton University, in Omaha, NE. She earned an MBA from the University of Houston, and started her own technical writing company. There she managed the writing of computer documentation and other types of procedure manuals.

After almost twenty years as a technical writer, Mary Ann went back to school to earn a Ph.D. in Religious Studies from Rice University, in Houston, Texas. Currently, she is a faculty member at Yavapai College in Prescott, Arizona where she teaches Comparative Religion.

As a recognized authority on the Afro-Caribbean religions, primarily Santería/Lukumi, she has published three academic books: *Then We Will Sing a New Song: African Influences on America's Religious Landscape* (Roman & Littlefield, 2012), *Santería: Correcting the Myths and Uncovering the Realities of a Growing Religion* (Praeger Publishers, 2007) and *Where Men are Wives and Mothers Rule: Santería Ritual Practices and Their Gender Implications* (University Press of Florida, 2005).

Her debut novella *The Baron's Box* (2017) was an account of one woman's journey through a surprising afterlife. *The Third Way*, the first novel in the Force of Destiny series, explores how to deal with a deadly threat without either capitulating or fighting back.

Connect with Mary Ann:

Blog: https://drmaryann.wordpress.com/musings/
Twitter: https://twitter.com/drmaryann
Facebook: https://www.facebook.com/mary.a.clark.395

Want to keep up with the latest Mary Ann Clark releases? Subscribe to her announcement list, http://eepurl.com/cVeMHf, to receive release-day alerts and news about special events and signings.

Made in the USA
Columbia, SC
17 March 2019